AN IRISHMAN
IN CHINA

This book is edited and designed by the Editorial Committee of *Cultural China* series

Text: Zhao Changtian
Translation: Yang Shuhui, Yang Yunqin
Cover image: Quanjing
Interior Designer: Xue Wenqing
Cover Designer: Wang Wei

Copy Editor: Kirstin Mattson
Editor: Wu Ying
Editorial Director: Zhang Yicong

Senior Consultants: Sun Yong, Wu Ying, Yang Xinci
Managing Director and Publisher: Wang Youbu

ISBN: 978-1-60220-238-2

Address any comments about *An Irishman in China: Robert Hart, Inspector General of the Chinese Imperial Maritime Customs* to:

Better Link Press
99 Park Ave
New York, NY 10016
USA

or

Shanghai Press and Publishing Development Company
F 7 Donghu Road, Shanghai, China (200031)
Email: comments_betterlinkpress@hotmail.com

Printed in China by Shenzhen Donnelley Printing Co., Ltd.

1   3   5   7   9   10   8   6   4   2

An Irishman in China

Robert Hart, Inspector General of the
Chinese Imperial Maritime Customs

Zhao Changtian
Translated by Yang Shuhui and Yang Yunqin

Better Link Press

Contents

Chapter One

The year is 1854 and we see no lighthouses or weather stations along the coast of China. They are yet to be set up, by the very man who, at this point in our story, is sailing by on a 150-ton schooner. Suffering from the torments of seasickness, he is half a world away from his hometown in Northern Ireland.

The concept of distance is relative to that of time. In this day and age with 21st century technology, it takes only about ten hours to travel from London to Hong Kong or to Shanghai, and the telephone and Internet transmit voice and images in the twinkling of an eye. But in 1854, after setting sail in May, it was a good seven weeks later, in July, that Robert Hart arrived in Hong Kong, after passing through Southampton, Alexandria, the Suez Canal and Ceylon. Once in Hong Kong, this nineteen-year-old young man, exhausted after bad bouts of sickness, felt that his long journey had truly taken him to another world.

But Hong Kong was not his final destination. Two months later, he set sail again, heading to Shanghai and then on to the coastal city of Ningbo, to take up his job as a student interpreter at the British Consulate there. Compared with his intercontinental journey two months earlier, this trip should not have been much of a challenge but young Hart had not been well-prepared mentally for it, and the 150-ton *Iona* was no large oceangoing vessel.

At dawn on September 15, the *Iona* ran into trouble soon after its sail was unfurled because with the wind shifting directions and blowing every which way, it was only on the second attempt that the ship got through the narrow channel between two small islands and left the harbor. By this time, the sun had risen, dyeing the never-ending sea a spectacular golden red. The young man on deck admiring the glorious sunrise thought that the stars dancing in front of his eyes were from the radiance of the sun, but when they showed no sign of fading, he realized that he was seasick.

The sea was in fact tolerably calm when he first got sick. It was five days later that a raging storm descended in full force. Wind-driven waves that spouted sky high crashed down like a collapsing wall and swept over the deck with the sharp bite of knives. The ship plunged into an abyss and, the next moment, was thrown atop the crest of another great swell. Pounded and squeezed by the mighty waves, the schooner looked as pathetic as a small leaf helplessly submitting itself to the ravages of the storm, likely to capsize, fall apart and perish at any moment.

Before the storm had sprung up, Hart had already been feeling ill for several days. His head in a swirl, he had lost track of time and felt too miserable to be even aware of any fear. He curled himself up in his small cabin, vomiting until there was nothing to throw up except bitter bile. No one paid him any attention, to say nothing of taking care of him. It was the *Iona* that needed all the attention there was to give. Luckily, his youth and energy sustained him through the tribulations until he gradually got used to the rises and falls of his world.

When the schooner finally drew near Dinghai and cast anchor at a spot within view of the distant coast, he got out of his cabin for the first time in many days. The wind had not subsided. A shower of red sand swept up from the bottom of the shoal and pounced on him, covering him with muddy sand from head to toe.

After only a brief stay, the schooner continued on its way along the coastline against the gale, stopping from time to time to replenish its supplies of fresh water and food, and to fix the frayed sailing ropes. One day, it had to berth at a notorious bay haunted by pirates, where three pirate ships had cast anchor only a few leagues away. Thanks to the strong winds and high waves, the pirates were too preoccupied with taking care of themselves to approach their prey. The storm plus the menace of piracy gave Hart the feeling of walking shoulder to shoulder with Death. He felt he had no reason to gamble with his young life, with the potential to lose all in an alien land. It was a huge stake with not much in terms of reward—he was to be nothing more than a humble supernumerary interpreter, a non-official member of the British Consular Service.

And so he began to have regrets. He wanted to go back home, but going home was by no means easy either. If he wished to leave China and return to his hometown, he would need to live frugally for an entire year, saving as much of his salary as possible in order to afford a second-class ticket to Northern Ireland. But even so, he had already made up his mind to go back as soon as he had enough money for the journey. He could return to his alma mater, Queen's College at Belfast,[1] to go on with his studies for a few years before becoming an attorney or a clergyman.

On the vast sea he often lost himself in memories, which became his means of escape from the prolonged nightmare. Everything was so appealing in those memories—the scenic Lagan Valley, the *broad straight road with high trees on either side* that *led up to Sam Jones's*[2], and the erudite professor of logic Dr. McCosh.[3] Hart had been an outstanding student and often placed first on examinations. So when the British Foreign Office asked Queens College for a nomination for the Consular Service in China, the Council of the College readily recommended him. In view of his excellent grades, the planned exam was dispensed with, and the only appointment allotted to the college was offered to this shy young man.

Holding a ticket to paradise, he now found himself suffering in hell. But who was to know what the future held?

Twenty-two days later, the *Iona* finally drew near the Wusongkou Delta. The wind had let up a week earlier, but Hart had already got used to tossing on the stormy sea and his mood had begun to improve. When he saw the verdant coastline of the mouth of the Yangzi River looming in the distance some moments earlier and heard the firing of a gun, the signal for the ship to "lay to," something like a surge of joy came over him.

Once he had been through inspections by British naval officers on duty at Shanghai's port of Wusongkou, he hurriedly put his belongings in order and proceeded up the Huangpu River in a boat belonging to Jardine, Matheson & Company. After it pulled up to the Bund Wharf, he crossed the floating bridge over the muddy foreshore and planted his feet on the macadam-paved street. As he stood there, he felt as if the ground was still shaking, as if he was still aboard the ship. He knew he was on solid ground but the sensation of the ship heaving and pitching stayed with him for a while.

"Lubin! Lubin!" James Mongan cried out Hart's Chinese name excitedly as he ran over to Hart. Mongan was also a student interpreter, recruited by the Foreign Office at about the same time. He had left Hong Kong one month earlier and been assigned to the British Consulate in Shanghai. "Lubin! Hurry up! Sir John Bowring is waiting for you!" he said as he took Hart's leather suitcase.

"Who? Sir John Bowring? He's waiting for me?" Hart couldn't quite believe his ears. Bowring was the new British Minister Plenipotentiary to China and the Governor of Hong Kong. Would he be so eager to greet a lowly student interpreter on arrival?

"Hurry up! I'm not kidding you! Don't you realize that because you've been on the sea for 22 days without sending a word, and what with the storm and the pirates, we all thought …"

"You all thought I was dead?"

"Sir John regrets not having told you to depart for Shanghai with him a few days earlier."

"I'm surprised myself that I'm still alive and kicking," said Hart. His sense of humor had returned.

"As the Chinese proverb puts it, this is a case of 'Da nan bu si, bi you hou fu' or 'Surviving a major disaster augurs good fortune in the future.'"

"I haven't heard that one," said Hart.

"I picked it up from Lay after I arrived in Shanghai."

"Who's Lay?"

"Horatio Nelson Lay is Vice Consul in the British Consulate in Shanghai. His command of the Chinese language is exceptional. You'll get to see him in a minute."

The British Consulate in Shanghai was housed in a fashionable new two-story red-tiled and white-walled structure. It stood right across from Hart and Mongan. On the spacious uncovered veranda were rattan tables and chairs set for afternoon tea. The newly planted trees were still small but the lawn was luxuriantly green.

The black iron gate was closed but the wicket door in the gate permitted access. Sikh guards wearing white turbans took Hart's luggage. Hart felt that he was being given special treatment indeed.

As they entered the second-floor lounge facing the Huangpu River, Sir John Bowring went up to greet him, saying, "Young man, you must have had a rough time."

Hart had met Bowring before, in Hong Kong. It was Bowring who had personally announced to him that he was to be transferred to Ningbo.

"Da nan bu si, bi you hou fu," said a thin and frail-looking man standing off to one side.

"That's Lay," whispered Mongan.

"Thank you," said Hart.

"You know what it means?" asked Lay.

"It's a Chinese proverb."

"Not bad!" said Bowring. "You've made rapid progress in your Chinese." Minister Bowring was a poet and a polyglot, said to be proficient in dozens of languages including Mandarin and Cantonese. After he introduced Hart to the officials present in proper order—Rutherford Alcock, British Consul in Shanghai, then Thomas Francis Wade, Commissioner of Customs, and finally Horatio Nelson Lay, Vice Consul in Shanghai—he said, "You may rest for a week in Shanghai and have them take you around for some sightseeing. But be careful. The county seat is now occupied by the Small Sword Society."

"The Small Sword Society?" This was the first time Hart had heard the name.

"I told you when we met in Hong Kong that last year, in Guangxi Province, a Christian named Hong Xiuquan had started an armed rebellion against the government and founded the Taiping Heavenly Kingdom."

"Are the Small Sword Society and the Taiping Heavenly Kingdom one and the same?"

"As far as we know, the Small Sword Society has no organizational ties with the Taipings but both are anti-government, and the Small Sword Society has developed on the strength of the Taiping Heavenly Kingdom."

"Are the members all natives of Shanghai?" asked Hart.

"No. Most of them are Cantonese and Fujianese," replied Bowring. "The British government maintains neutrality vis-à-vis the insurgents and the Qing government. We do not intervene in Chinese domestic affairs. So foreigners are safe here but one still needs to take care. Even before the Small Sword Society insurgency, public order in the city was deplorable. Almost all the scoundrels of the world are gathered here." Noticing Hart's puzzled look, Bowring continued, "Lay will tell you more about the details of the situation in Shanghai and in your destination, Ningbo. He's an old China hand. We've been extremely busy these last few days." With that, he left with Alcock and Wade, leaving Hart with Lay and Mongan.

Lay said, "Your Chinese is not bad. You even know the proverb, 'Da nan bu si, bi you hou fu.'"

"Actually," Hart hastened to explain, "I just picked it up from Mongan."

"And I just picked it up from …" Mongan cast Lay a glance.

Lay said with a smile, "Chinese is a very interesting language. Work hard at it!"

"But it's very difficult."

"You need to put your brain to work rather than just trying to memorize everything. Chinese characters are pictograms with set patterns to their formation." Lay went on to cite an example: "Let's take the character for man," he said, tracing the symbol 男. "Look, the upper part, or radical, is the character for 'field,' and the lower one is for 'strength.'"Assuming the posture of a laborer, he continued, "One who works hard in the field—a man."

"But why is 'field' written in this way?" asked Hart.

"It's a pictogram! Isn't this a picture of four square fields?"

"What about 'strength'?"

"That's even more interesting. Look at the bend on the right-hand side. Isn't it like a bending arm?" Bending an arm, he continued, "The left stroke represents a kicking leg."

"Ah yes!" exclaimed Hart. "This is indeed interesting! Then what about the character for 'woman'?"

Lay dipped a finger in his tea and traced the character 女 on the table with his finger. "What does it look like to you?" he asked.

"It looks like a woman dancing."

"That's one way to look at it."

"What are other ways to look at it?"

"This is the head, these are two hands, two feet, and in the middle is a hole."

"A hole?"

"Let me ask you: How are men and women different?"

Hart's face froze, and Lay burst out laughing. "I thought you were a virgin. I'm surprised that you do know what it is. All right, now let's take a look at the city of Shanghai."

They stepped onto the balcony through open French windows flanked by white lace curtains fluttering in the breeze. The wide Huangpu River was dotted by sailboats. To the north was another river, narrower than the Huangpu but equally busy with traffic. "That's the Wusong River," said Lay. "It leads up to Suzhou, Hangzhou, Huzhou and Jiaxing—all of them abound in rice, silk and tea. Those are the backyards of Shanghai and make up the richest region of China. That's why Shanghai is so vital to the British Empire. It's the most important port of China. Now look in the other direction," said Lay as he pointed at a building to the south. "That's the French Consulate. Next to it is another body of water called Yangjing Creek. It's narrower than the Wusong River but is also open to navigation. Further to the south is the seat of the County of Shanghai."

"So we're outside of the city proper?"

"Yes. This used to be an uninhabited swamp." With a look of contempt, Lay continued, "It's very short-sighted of the Chinese government to lease to foreigners what they take to be a useless piece of land. We see it as the best part of Shanghai. Look! This is the point of convergence of the Huangpu and Wusong, the two largest rivers of Shanghai. It's the hub of China's inland navigation and, as such, will naturally become the most important and the most glamorous place in Shanghai. What's more, the cannons of our warships are within firing range and can effectively ensure our safety."

Hart kept nodding, deeply convinced by Lay's logic. With his boyish face Lay looked like he was only twenty years old but his insights and his tone showed maturity and experience way beyond his years. Sir John Bowring called him an "old China hand," and it was nothing short of a miracle for such a young man to be referred to in this way.

"Sir John said a moment ago that almost all the scoundrels

of the world are gathered here," said Hart. "Why is that?"

Lay explained, "According to the 1842 Nanjing Treaty, Shanghai and Ningbo are both open trading ports but the Chinese Customs is too corrupt. You know, officials of the Chinese Customs are paid meager salaries but they are all flush with cash. That's simply due to taking bribes. There's nothing easier than greasing their palms. Therefore, in this place, as long as you have money, anything is possible. A little bit of bribery can bring a windfall. That's why this place attracts adventurers and, yes, scoundrels, from all over the world. Anyone without a sense of morality can strike it rich here—immensely rich. I suspect that there are any number of fugitives from the law among them, because this is their best safe haven."

"Doesn't the Chinese Emperor know about this? Why doesn't he stop them?"

"The imperial court is aware but they lack the means to stop them. So they asked us, the British Consulate, to help them stop English merchants from smuggling."

"Are we going to help them?"

"According to the provisions of the Nanjing Treaty, we have the obligation to urge British merchants to pay taxes to the Chinese Customs. Taking a long view, we also wish to establish normalized trade. We don't want the city to become a paradise for criminals. The interests of the British Empire must be safeguarded by law and order.

"The problem is that when the Chinese officials themselves engage in fraudulent activities, our admonitions to British merchants don't work. Plus, only Britain has such an agreement with China. The consulates of other countries have no such obligations. This means that Britain is at a disadvantage in our trade with China, and this inequality weakens our trading power. It obviously doesn't make sense that British merchants can't engage in smuggling while French, American and Portuguese merchants do so without restraint."

Having just arrived in China, Hart found himself yet unable to grasp such complex issues. Turning to another matter, he asked, "Why do we stay neutral in the conflict between the government and the rebelling peasants?"

"Because we don't know yet who will come out the winner. We must leave enough leeway for future British actions in China."

Hart took his meals at Lay's home while lodging with Mongan. Lay's younger brother William Hyde Lay was a junior assistant at the British Consulate in Shanghai. Now only in their twenties, the brothers had come to China with their father, a diplomat, in their early teens and acquired proficiency in Chinese. In the British diplomatic service, with its dire scarcity of Chinese-speaking officials, they were quickly promoted to high positions.

After dinner, Mongan took Hart out for a walk. "Shall I take you on a little tour of the city?" asked Mongan.

"By all means!"

They headed south along the riverside. Before reaching Yangjing Creek, they came within view of the walls of Shanghai County. The walls were somewhat similar to those of Scottish castles, only they were built not of stone but of thick grey bricks. A swath of stains left by fire and smoke was visible on the moss-covered walls. One of the two panels of the arched northern gate was standing open, and two rebel guards stood by, carrying sophisticated-looking firearms. No one was going in or out.

"Can we go in?" Hart asked.

Mongan replied, "The Chinese are not allowed to go in or out freely. Foreigners can."

"Isn't it strange that foreigners enjoy greater freedom of movement than the Chinese on Chinese territory?"

"There's nothing strange about it," said Mongan. "The rebels want our support. In fact their firearms are supplied by our merchants."

"Why?" Hart was puzzled. "Why do our British

merchants supply them with arms?" "That's politics. I don't know the exact ins and outs of it all, but this much I know—it's all a matter of interests."

This being his first time in an ancient Chinese city, Hart was overwhelmed by the exotic sights and he found everything a novelty. As he was looking all around him, he heard Mongan call out, "Hey! Mr. Wylie!" Hart followed the direction of Mongan's gaze and saw a middle-aged Caucasian wearing a Chinese-style cotton gown. Introducing him, Mongan explained that Wylie was an English linguist well-versed not only in Chinese but also in Russian, Mongolian and many other languages, and that, as an employee of the London Mission Press, he was now engaged in the translation and printing of a Chinese version of the Bible. Awed by the man's knowledge and his work, Hart eagerly made a respectful bow. Wylie said with a wave of his hand, "Don't stand on ceremony with me, young man. Welcome to China! Let me be your guide. I'll take you to the City Temple first."

The City Temple was just a few steps away. It had a spacious courtyard overhung with multi-colored flags fluttering in the wind. A slightly raised path led to a building with a yellow brick tile roof, red walls and upturned eaves. On each side of the gate squatted a fierce-looking granite lion. As they stepped over the high threshold, they were met by the scent of incense, which permeated the hall.

Wylie then took them to a long, narrow sandalwood table on which stood conical boxes, open at one end, with bamboo slips in them. An old woman took a box and shook it until one of the bamboo strips fell out. Quickly she picked it up, held it piously as she approached an old man sitting off to one side, and respectfully handed the slip to him. Wylie explained in a subdued voice, "This is a temple to the god who runs this city. Chinese Daoists worship a multiplicity of gods and the city god is one of them. The old woman is asking for a divination, hoping for divine revelation of her destiny."

"How is the divination done?"

"First, she shows the priest the bamboo slip. The priest will then find in his book a passage corresponding to the number of the slip. It's usually an unpunctuated poem. This is what inspires the priest as he tells her fortune."

"Is there any truth to the divinations?" asked a puzzled Hart.

Wylie replied with a smile, "Of course not, but the Chinese believe there is. They say sometimes the divinations are very accurate."

Hart took a box and shook it just out of curiosity, with half a mind to find out about his own destiny in China. But then, at the thought that this was un-Christian, he put the box back.

After they left the temple, Wylie said, "Let me take you to another interesting place." They ducked into a narrow and dirty winding alley lined with shops, mostly closed. The few shops that were open had few customers. At a place that resembled a shop, Wylie stopped and said, "This place specializes in buying paper with characters on them, at three cents per pound. They also buy chinaware with characters stamped on them."

"What do they do with the paper and the chinaware?" asked Hart.

"They don't put them to use. The waste paper is burnt; the broken crockery is taken to the sea by boats and thrown overboard."

"Why?" Hart looked at Wylie, mystified.

"The Chinese have such a reverence for their written characters that they destroy everything stamped with them, so that the characters are not dishonored in any way."

"Oh, what a civilized nation this is! They reverence letters more than piety."[4]

"Yes," said Wylie. "I share your views."

All of a sudden, Hart was overwhelmed with a feeling of respect for this seemingly backward country.

In the following few days, Horatio Lay's younger brother

William and Mongan continued to take Hart sightseeing in and around Shanghai.

Shanghai was indeed a unique city. The original walled city had already been highly prosperous before it was opened to foreign trade in 1844. But it was now occupied by the Small Swords Society rebels, and although no curfew had been imposed, business was slack because rich inhabitants had been fleeing the city.

The north section near the International Settlement and the west section near the French Concession used to be busy marketplaces but had been burned in the seesaw battles between the rebels and the government army led by the Circuit Intendant, or Daotai, of Shanghai. There were now nothing but dirty tumble-down sheds for displaced persons and garbage piled up like hills.

North of Yangjing Creek was the first piece of land that had been rented out to foreigners back in 1844. Within a short space of ten years, more than 120 foreign mercantile establishments had settled there. Stretching south from the British Consulate by the Wusong River were Jardine, Matheson & Company, London's Peninsular and Oriental Steam Navigation Company, Sassoon & Co., Gibb Livingston & Co., Augustine Heard & Co., Shaw Brothers & Co., Dent & Co., Turner & Co., Smith, Kennedy & Co., Russell & Co., Wheelock & Co., Adamson & Co., and H. Fogg & Company.

The buildings that housed these companies stood in one row, in varying heights, all facing the Huangpu River. Around the buildings were spacious, tidy and beautiful gardens with roses and lilacs. Behind these buildings stood a row of upscale residential houses with gardens, some still under construction. Englishmen in these surroundings would feel quite at home, as if in their own country, if not for the fact that every house was so new and splendid that they might as well be in a fairyland.

To the west lay rows of newly put up wooden structures. Built in haste in less than a year, they were shabby and packed closely together, forming quite a contrast to the lovely nearby houses. William Lay told Hart that according to regulations, Chinese residents were not allowed in the foreign settlements. However after the Taiping troops occupied Nanjing a year earlier, rich landowners and merchants in the southern part of Jiangsu had been fleeing to Shanghai to seek refuge in the foreign settlements. Because there were too many of them, and most of them were rich with all kinds of connections, the government could hardly stop them.

This presented foreign merchants living in the settlements with a splendid opportunity to make money. In haste, they constructed more than 800 wooden houses and offered them to the Chinese refugees for rent at a high price. In less than three months the wooden houses were all snatched up.

Previously the settlements were quiet and clean all right, but there had been so few people and stores that daily life there was most inconvenient. Now that so many rich Chinese with strong purchasing power had made it into the settlements, the markets blossomed instantly and became filled with Chinese customers who sported expensive jewelry and had none of the sorry looks usually associated with refugees.

After supper one evening, Hart went for a walk with William Mongan near the horse racing course by the Wusong River. The newly arrived rich Chinese refugees had not yet taken up horse racing as a means of recreation, so it was still a quiet place. It was a clear and crisp autumn evening. Amid the cool, soothing breezes from the green turf of the racing course, a horse-carriage passed them from behind and pulled up at the stands. From the carriage stepped a lady whose youthful and charming profile immediately caught Hart's attention.

She was Caucasian, wearing a white silk dress as smooth and shiny as fox fur and tailored so well that it hugged her every contour. She walked with an airy step, her full hips under her narrow waist swaying alluringly. Hart found his eyes glued on her. It was not until she had disappeared through the gate of the racing course that Hart gathered his senses.

William Lay gave him a knowing nudge on the elbow and said, "Why don't we go somewhere for a little fun? They've got everything here." Judging from Lay's furtive look, Hart realized he had forgotten his manners in staring so long, and hastened to shake his head.

"But it's all right," insisted Lay. "They've got places exclusively for foreigners. All the women are Westerners. They don't have such places in Ningbo." Hart still shook his head in firm rejection.

John Meadows, Vice Consul of the British Consulate in Ningbo, went personally to the dock to greet Hart. This broad, tall Caucasian looked conspicuous in the crowds of Chinese around him. He had on a snuff-colored coat and a pair of white trousers. His hair was a dark sandy color mingled with grey, and he sported a French-style beard. Hart had spotted him from afar, thinking that he must be Mr. Meadows, because Hart knew that Meadows was the only Englishman in the British Consulate in Ningbo. All the other employees were Chinese.

But when he walked up to Meadows, the latter did not even see him, much less greet him, not realizing that the young man he was here to meet was right in front of him. As Meadows kept sweeping the crowd with his eyes, Hart walked past him without acknowledgment. He did mean to say hello but his voice failed him. He realized the absurdity of it. Of course he should have taken the initiative and asked, "Might you be the British Consul, sir?" There was no one else he could be. And yet, he had gone past Meadows.

He hated himself for his shyness, and asked himself, "What am I going to do now? How am I going to locate the British Consulate?" Of course, Ningbo was not a big city and there must be a Union Jack flying over the British Consulate. He should be able to find it. But once in the consulate, wouldn't he still have to say hello to this bearded Consul all the same? Wouldn't it be even more ridiculous and embarrassing for him? He slowed down and braced himself to turn back and greet the man. But by this time Meadows had overtaken him, and with a bow, asked, "Might you be Mr. Hart?"

Happily, Hart returned the bow and said, "Mr. Meadows, I presume?"

Laughing heartily, Meadows said, "There's a Chinese proverb that says, 'One who may be as far away as the sky is in fact right in front of your eyes.' I was scanning the sky for you and forgot to check what was right before my eyes."

Greatly relieved, Hart also smiled, thinking, "The Chinese language is indeed interesting."

The British Consulate was housed in a white-walled and black roof-tiled Chinese-style residential compound in Yangjia Lane a little back from the river. It was quite a run-down place with yellow water stains, grayish splotches of grime and age-old moss on the white walls. There were two courtyards, one behind the other, where weeds were left to grow in clumps out of the cracks in the brick pavement. There was also a garden in the back with no flowers, just a few trees and patches of luxuriant weeds.

Hart was put up in an east-facing room off the second courtyard.

"Is the room all right?" asked Meadows.

The room was actually quite shabby, nothing like the British Consulate in Shanghai, but Hart replied, "It's fine."

"My room is right opposite yours but sometimes I don't stay here." Meadows gave a naughty wink as he said this, a gesture that Hart found quite incongruous with his status and his age. "The Consulate has a Chinese gatekeeper who sleeps in that small room by the gate. I suggest that you hire a cleaning boy and a cook, each for only four dollars per month. Your monthly salary is seventy-two dollars, enough to cover all your expenses."

"How much does it cost to engage a Chinese teacher?"

"Not much, either. Seven dollars."

"Could you help me hire a cook, a cleaning boy and a Chinese teacher?"

"Sure, no problem. I've already ordered supper for you. It will be delivered to you but it's Chinese food. We can't find any cooks of Western cuisine in Ningbo, because there are very few Westerners here, unlike Hong Kong or Shanghai. Apart from the two of us and two officials in the Portuguese Consulate, there are only a few foreign merchants and about a dozen missionaries and their wives. Oh, there's also a Miss Aldersey who doesn't belong to any religious group. She's a spinster in her fifties. She paid her own way to China and has leased a large compound in the center of the town for the girls' school she established."

"A missionary school?"

"Yes. Who else would want to come to China except missionaries?" Laughing, he continued, "Oh, yes—except us! Mr. Hart, are you religious?"

"Of course."

"Sorry! Too bad I am not. So they are always on guard against me. And now they'll be afraid that I'm going to corrupt you."

Hart was at a loss for a reply. Meadows continued, "But I'll take you to call on them first thing tomorrow morning. They'll be glad to see you."

In the evening, Meadows disappeared, and the Chinese old gatekeeper turned off his lights and went to bed early. The entire compound was engulfed in darkness. The dim light emitted by the flickering flame of the kerosene lamp on the table was quickly swallowed by the darkness. Unexpectedly there came from outside the crisp sound of something striking on wood. Hart was puzzled, learning only later that the sound came from a night watchman striking the hour, a sound that only accentuated the stillness of the night. This place was no Hong Kong or Shanghai. For the first time, Hart was hit by a sense of the loneliness of a foreigner in a strange land.

The next day brought Hart a pleasant surprise that exceeded all his expectations. He was at the home of R. Q. Way, a missionary of the American Presbyterian Church. Mr.

Way was not at home, so Meadows and Hart were received by his wife who was quite a delight to the eyes. She introduced to Hart another guest who happened to be there: Miss Dyer, teacher at Aldersey's Girls' School. In fact, Miss Dyer had caught Hart's eye the moment he entered the house but he had looked away, not wanting to get caught staring at the absolutely gorgeous young lady.

He had never expected to see in an unknown Chinese town an English girl as beautiful as a fairy maiden. Actually, the analogy was a bit trite and not very accurate either. She was not only gorgeous but also lovely in a sort of soul-snatching way. Yes, Hart had a literary bent, and was confident in his articulateness, but in the presence of Miss Dyer, his eloquence failed him.

They sat down for tea—authentic Ceylon tea served with homemade cookies that were crispy but a little hard. However it was quite remarkable that they could enjoy such a treat in this place. Miss Dyer asked Hart excitedly, "Have you just arrived from England?"

Hart replied, looking at the floor, "It's been almost six months since I left England. I spent most of that time on the voyage."

"Ah yes, England is so far from here. I would really like to know the latest fashion in London."

"Sorry, I don't know anything about fashion," said Hart as he raised his eyes to look at Miss Dyer. But just as quickly he shifted his eyes to the vibrantly yellow chrysanthemums on the windowsill. He cursed himself for not having the courage to keep his eyes on Miss Dyer, to look at her with self-assurance. But that brief glance was enough for him to take in her splendor.

Ningbo was not a big city, and the missionaries basically all lived in the same neighborhood, so Meadows and Hart completed their round of visits to about a dozen of the families in one day. Each family cordially welcomed the good-looking young Irishman. But his thoughts were always with Miss Dyer.

By that evening, he still regretted not having expanded on the topic of London fashion. Even though he was a stranger to London, he had been interviewed there by Mr. Hammond, Under Secretary of the Foreign Office, right before his departure. For a nineteen-year-old man, that was beyond any doubt an experience to brag about, and it surely would have impressed Miss Dyer. His introversion had cost him many opportunities, especially with girls. In his last few months at Queen's College, he had been compelled by the desires of the flesh and ended up frequenting the pleasure quarters, where relationships were a business transaction. The reason for this was that he was still unable to derive pleasure from associations with the other sex through any sort of normal channels. He detested his shyness and reticence.

Without his previous experience in houses of ill repute, he would not have been in such agony now. But having had intimacy with women, he knew that the pleasure a woman could give him was something irreplaceable. Every day he prayed for God to give him enough strength to resist temptation. He had been celibate for six months but the abstention only whetted his desire.

As he lay in bed in the darkness, Miss Dyer's image remained before him, however hard he tried to drive it away. Dressed in finery, she was smiling in her graceful and elegant manner. "Would she be willing to marry me?" Hart asked himself. If she were to be his future wife, he thought he would be *reconciled to Ningbo.*[5]

Even though it was only a two-person affair, the consulate in Ningbo still represented the British Empire and, in accordance with Chinese custom, it demanded a display of dignity worthy of a British Consulate. Meadows and Hart hired two sedans with four men carrying each chair. Two men wearing caps, to which small English flags were attached, ran ahead to clear the way. One man walked behind; he was the chief attendant who bore and presented their cards.

They soon arrived at the Circuit Intendant's yamen.[6] They got out of the sedan chairs in the parking hall and, after crossing several courts, reached the spacious front yard, which was flanked by an honor guard beating gongs and playing wind instruments. Amid the noise of the firecrackers, the Circuit Intendant and two lower-ranking officials stood in waiting at the front door of the reception room. The Circuit Intendant, a portly old man wearing fashionable imported spectacles, politely led them into the room.

Hart was then seated to the right of the Circuit Intendant and Meadows to the left. Tea, refreshments, wine and various delicacies were served in a fine spread. The Circuit Intendant placed several little tidbits from each of the dishes on the small plate in front of Hart. He noticed that the Circuit Intendant had long nails on his short and thick fingers, and that the nails were dirty. Though a little uncomfortable at the sight, he knew that to be served personally by such a distinguished Chinese official was a great honor. He also noticed that the Circuit Intendant helped him before helping Meadows, which made him feel uneasy.

Wine glasses were used for Shaoxing rice wine, which looked like whiskey in color but of course was completely different in taste. The Circuit Intendant raised his glass, waved it in a graceful manner and said, "Ganbei!" Hart took only a sip but the Circuit Intendant drained his own glass in one gulp, turning the glass upside down to prove that he had finished the last drop. As he burst out laughing, an attendant immediately went up to refill his glass. Hart's glass was emptied and also refilled to the brim.

In the second round of drinking, Hart followed the Circuit Intendant's example and finished his glass in one gulp, to the applause of the Chinese officials. Meadows told Hart that "ganbei" meant one had to finish up the wine in the glass, and that in their tradition, the more their guests drank, the happier were the hosts. Hart said, "My father used to own a distillery. I've been drinking since my earliest years. I can drink as much as they want me to."

Meadows turned to the Circuit Intendant and said, "Mr. Hart just said that he liked your wine." The Circuit Intendant said with delight, "We have even better kinds. Come! Serve Luzhou liquor!" Attendants brought out small white porcelain cups and filled them with the liquor. Hart then called out, "Ganbei!" Throwing his head back, he finished his cup. Amidst general applause, everyone came up to toast him.

After returning to the consulate, Meadows praised Hart, saying "That was the best party we've ever had. With your drinking capacity, we'll have no problems dealing with the Chinese."

Hart replied, "That much liquor is nothing to an Irishman. But they seemed to have treated me as the more honored guest. Did you let them know about my status? I'm just a student interpreter, not a proper diplomat."

"Do you know what my status is?" asked Meadows, smiling.

"Vice Consul."

"No, I'm also just an interpreter. There's no consul here. I'm the only one in this consulate so of course I'm the man who calls the shots. I represent Britain. And the same now goes for you. You are one of the two diplomats of the British Consulate, so now you also call the shots. Remember, don't think of yourself as a student interpreter. No. You are a plenipotentiary of the British Empire in Ningbo."

Nodding, Hart said, "I'll keep that in mind, but I still shouldn't be placed ahead of you."

Meadows burst out laughing. "Do you know what they call me?"

"They? Who are 'they'?"

"Those missionaries. They call me—no, in fact, I call myself—a freethinker."

"A freethinker?"

"Yes. I'm not their kind. By 'they,' I mean not only the missionaries but also those officials."

"I'm not sure what you mean, Mr. Meadows."

"Take you and me for example. I came to China earlier than you did. I am an interpreter and you are a student interpreter, but I don't think I should walk and talk and be toasted ahead of you. No. I don't care about those things. It doesn't have to be that way. I don't like rigid rules. I told you that I'm not religious, but that doesn't mean I don't have faith. I worship God. It's the rigid formalities and rules of the church that put me off. Belief in God is a matter of the heart, rather than something for show. Many of those people who kneel piously in front of the cross behave worse than beasts. I've seen too many of such cases."

"There is certainly something in what you say," conceded Hart.

"No, not just 'something,' but 'much truth.' Let me tell you another thing. Even if I don't, you'll get wind of it soon enough. They will tell you about it so as to stop me from corrupting you. I have a Chinese wife."

"A Chinese wife?" said Hart in astonishment.

"Actually it's not a very accurate expression, although, yes, I have only one wife and she is Chinese. But they refer to her as my mistress."

"Why?"

"Because we are not technically married, or, in other words, we have not gone through the proper formalities. It's not that we don't want to. There's just no way we can go about it. But I treat her entirely as wife. After I die, all my property goes to her."

"Mr. Meadows, it's too early for you to talk about death."

"True, but I must make this clear."

"You are a high-minded person indeed, Mr. Meadows," said Hart from the bottom of his heart.

When introducing the Chinese teacher to Hart, Meadows did not mention his name. He said only that he was a teacher, and since he had passed the imperial civil service examinations at the provincial level, his ranking as a "juren" was equivalent to a college professorship in England. His name was indeed of no importance, since it was only proper to address him as "Teacher."

The teacher's voice was heavily guttural. Hart watched his lips intently to imitate his speech. As for what he was saying, Hart was at a loss. It was an outrageous idea to make two people who did not understand each other sit together as teacher and student. However the idea seemed to be acceptable to both parties. On Hart's part, it was out of the lack of choice. But why did the teacher accept the job? What prowess did he have to make his student acquire mastery of the language?

It turned out that while the Chinese teacher was not an interesting person, a session with him was the least boring part of Hart's day. They tried to express themselves through every possible means at their disposal—gesticulating, imitating with body movement or voice, and assuming exaggerated facial expressions. Watching this mild-mannered man in his fifties stooping low, bending his legs, squinting his eyes, and meowing like a cat or oinking like a pig, Hart could hardly stifle a giggle.

And yet, however fun it was, Chinese was so difficult to learn, a hundred times more so than French. Sometimes Hart thought, why bother to take such pains to improve his proficiency if he was to return home as early as next year?

Hart's motivation for continuing with his study of Chinese, therefore, was simply from the lack of something better to do. It was impossible to go back home right away. He simply could not afford it. So he had to do something to kill time. His shipment of books from Ireland had not arrived, and he had finished reading the few books he had brought with him. He could not, for the life of him, come up with another way to keep himself amused.

After the teacher departed, he was left all alone with no one to talk to. Meadows was often away, presumably with his Chinese wife. Meadows was busy having a boat built so that he could make a home there, which Hart found to be a romantic idea. He thought, "They say it's not expensive to have a boat made. Should I also have one built? But what fun would it be if I stay on it all by myself?" Drifting down the river to take in scenery would certainly call for female companionship.

Female companionship was something Hart longed for, in his loneliness. He could have visited the missionaries at their homes. They would have welcomed him with open arms and they had indeed issued him invitations. He could have gone to chat with the men and look at the women. He yearned for female society, yet he was afraid of being with them and watching them live happily with their men. He could go to visit Miss Dyer. He was sure she would not reject him, but he had no idea what to say to her. He felt himself incapable of mouthing empty words, but what matters of substance could he discuss with Miss Dyer?

He had seriously weighed the option of proposing to Miss Dyer. He could very well ask Meadows to convey the message, and was sure that Meadows would be happy to render this service. Miss Dyer would most probably give her consent. But what next? Would he be able to support an English wife? He would need a house, a bevy of servants, and butter, raisins, strawberry jam and biscuits from England. This was the lifestyle of every foreign family here, a lifestyle that was beyond his means at this stage of his life. Since it was completely out of reach, what was the point of paying her visits? Hart was ever a man of reason.

Soon summer rolled around, preceded by a long stretch of "plum days," so called because it was the season when plums ripened. The weather on plum days was highly unpredictable: rain one moment and sunshine the next, or even rain and sunshine at the same time. Hart lived on the ground floor of an old house that was damp even when it was not raining. On plum days, the walls seemed covered in teardrops. The clothes in the leather trunks got mildewed, and one's skin was sticky and clammy all the time. He longed for the end of the plum days but Meadows told him that would herald the height of summer. In fact, English people should be accustomed to damp weather, but they still found the heat of Ningbo's summer quite unbearable.

One day, Captain Patridge came to the Consulate to request "port clearance," for Hart had by this time been given the charge of shipping and postal affairs. After going through the necessary formalities, he availed himself of the opportunity to have a chat with the captain. It was on Captain Patridge's sailboat the *Erin* that he had come to Ningbo last autumn, and he had subsequently seen quite a lot of the captain, so they could qualify as friends.

Talking about Ningbo's weather, Captain Patridge said, "The doors and windows of Chinese houses are too small with too little ventilation. Winter is not a problem but it's suffocating in summer. You'd be better off staying in my house. Mine is an English-style house with floor-to-ceiling windows and a balcony. It's very comfortable in the summer with breezes from the sea. And I've got a lot of vacant rooms."

Hart knew that Patridge doubled as an agent for Jardine & Matheson and also had a hand in opium trafficking. With his deep pockets, an extra person's room and board would not make any difference to him, and his invitation was sincere enough. So, after a few polite words of demurral, Hart agreed, much to Patridge's delight. Hart was also delighted because he had been unbearably lonely.

The following day, Patridge sent over a horse-carriage along with four porters to bring Hart into his mansion. Hart had no idea of the significance that day—July 2, 1855—was to have. It was then that he met Ayao, a Chinese woman, daughter of a boatman.

Pretty, healthy, full of life and charming, she had none of the reservations of a well brought-up girl of an elite Chinese family. In Ningbo, it was an honor for a girl from the lowest stratum of society to be able to attract a Westerner. Ayao started out being just curious about the young, good-looking and gentle-mannered foreigner of high status who, amazingly enough, could speak some Chinese. Her forwardness disarmed the shy and introverted Hart. His yearning for female companionship was becoming too much for him to bear. He had been abstaining for too long, the nightmarish venereal disease of the brothels of Ireland holding him back.

Ayao's vivaciousness and lack of sophistication dispelled his fears. In no time he was smitten. Living a celibate life for so long, he was unable to hold back. His appeal was such that no woman could resist.

Captain Patridge, being a sensible man, never took advantage of this relationship, or the favors he had done Hart, to ask for special treatment in shipping matters. Nor was he out to grease Hart's palm. They were just friends. Any official business was dealt with in the Consulate in the proper way. Of course, it was sometimes hard to draw the line and, in cases where the line was not all that clear-cut, Hart naturally chose not to make things difficult for his friend.

Before long, Hart was promoted to assistant interpreter. Since there was only one Vice Consul at the Ningbo consulate in charge of all consular affairs, the assistant interpreter was in fact the other Vice Consul. While Ningbo was no Shanghai, it was one of the five treaty ports after all. And as the Chinese saying goes, "The sparrow may be small but it has all the vital organs." Over the last two years, Hart had learned all the ins and outs of a consul's job and had passed the most difficult stage in his study of the Chinese language. He no longer entertained the idea of returning to Northern Ireland. Of course, the main reason for his disinclination was the thought of leaving Ayao. By now they were already living as man and wife.

The massive granite city wall, overgrown with dark green ivy, had turned gray with the ravages of time. The wide and flat top of the wall was more impressive than any of the streets in the city but there were few pedestrians, except for a few soldiers on patrol and an occasional beggar or two.

Hart and W. M. Martin had gone around the six-mile-long city wall on their horses several times at a gallop. When they had thoroughly enjoyed themselves, they slowed down and rode abreast with lax reins.

Martin was a missionary with the North American Presbyterian Church and had arrived in Ningbo in 1850 to do missionary work. After more than six years there, he had just been hired in June 1857, as a Chinese interpreter by the first US Minister in China. Upon Hart's first arrival in Ningbo three years earlier, Martin was the very first missionary to call on him, and the two of them had kept up their visits from time to time. And now, upon hearing that Martin was about to leave Ningbo, Hart went in haste to say goodbye.

"To be able to work for Minister William Bradford Reed as an interpreter is an excellent opportunity," said Hart with heartfelt admiration.

"Yes, I think so, too, which was why I volunteered for it. In Tianjin and Beijing, I'll get to know more people and so I'll have more opportunities to do my missionary work."

"That's true. Ningbo is quite out-of-the-way."

"But I have good feelings about Ningbo," said Martin. "It's a quiet place."

Hart nodded. "It's good as a place to live but there's very little room for career development."

"You have nothing to worry about," said Martin. "You are young and you have a promising career ahead of you. Plenty of opportunities will come your way and you are making good progress with your Chinese. In China, a Westerner with a good command of the Chinese language will have no lack of opportunities."

"It's indeed quite a challenge for a Westerner to learn Chinese. It's so difficult."

Martin laughed and said, "I remember when I first came to Ningbo, after I studied Chinese for about two months, my wife wanted me to ask our cook to buy eighteen bayberries.

The cook was gone for the longest time. After he finally returned, out of breath, carrying a basketful of sheep tails on his back, he said, "Sorry, I looked up and down the market but found only twelve sheep tails."

Hart also burst out laughing. "Ningbo dialect is so different from Mandarin," said he. "I tried to learn the Ningbo dialect but then gave it up."

"You have no need for the Ningbo dialect. As a diplomat, you won't stay in one place for long. It's different with us missionaries."

"Did you plan to stay in Ningbo on a long-term basis?"

"Yes, I did. I really admire Miss Aldersey. You know who she is. Just think: A frail, unmarried woman without any particular religious affiliation came to Ningbo more than ten years ago, when there were few missionaries in China. Before coming to China, she had stayed at home taking care of her sick father. It was only after her father passed away when she was forty that she took up missionary work and began to learn Chinese. And what a challenge it was for her to establish a school exclusively with her own funds! She kept at her work for more than ten years. You can still tell that she used to be quite good looking. She was not without suitors but her thoughts are entirely taken up by her missionary work. A missionary needs a meticulous, down-to-earth approach in doing God's will, setting up schools and hospitals to serve local populations."

"I have a great deal of respect for you, and for Miss Aldersey."

"We are very happy with the choices we've made. Do you know that Miss Aldersey takes a walk at five o'clock every morning on the city wall?"

"But it's still dark at five in winter."

"It's five o'clock sharp in winter, too, with a servant in front lighting her way with a lantern."

"She does have strength of character."

"Anyone with clearly defined goals for life and career will acquire strength of character. Lubin, the way I see it, your career success lies in China. You already have a good command of the Chinese language. Ningbo may not be a big city but, you've undoubtedly heard before, 'The sparrow may be small but it has all the vital organs.' The experience you've accumulated in the Ningbo Consulate will stand you in good stead in your future diplomatic career in China."

"You've been living here for six years now," said Hart. "How do you see China?"

"The Chinese are a great people. They are cultured, polite, hardworking, frugal, meek, friendly and soft on the outside but firm on the inside. Their current problem is that they know too little about the West, and they lack a business tradition and Western advanced technology. They need to change their views of the West and reform their system."

"Yes," Hart agreed. "Their relationship with the Western powers is tense at this stage, but in fact, Western countries have no other wish than to trade with China and develop normal trade relations."

"No," Martin shook his head. "Western countries' trade with China, especially in the case of your country, Britain, is mostly the opium trade. I oppose trading in opium, with all its great perils."

"I agree with you, but opium is also grown in China. I heard that opium-refining was actually invented in China."

"But cultivation of opium in China was controlled and was for medical purposes only. British merchants caused its proliferation."

"That was the work of some lawless merchants only."

Martin again shook his head. "It may appear that way, but those merchants have power in your Parliament. China exports tea, silk and other things in demand in the West, but China has no need for Western merchandise. They can fulfill their own needs. So more and more silver flows from the West to China, leading to trade imbalances. The only thing that can balance the trade is opium."

"It's very difficult to completely ban the opium trade.

The key to controlling the opium trade lies with the Chinese Customs, but it is in a terrible shape. Its door is almost wide open."

Martin rejoined, "That is why I believe that Western countries should help the Chinese in this regard. You diplomats have important responsibilities."

"So what do you think are the most important things to watch out for in China?"

Martin ruminated for a while before he answered, "The Chinese put a lot of value on considerations of 'face,' or dignity. This should be borne in mind first and foremost when dealing with the Chinese. They don't give as much weight to practical interests as Westerners do. For example, when it comes to offering gifts, the practical value of the gift is not as important as its pure monetary value. What means more to them is the 'face' of the recipient. It's a gift of 'face,' really."

"Right. I've heard when a Chinese official is found guilty of crime and is sentenced to death, if he can be allowed to wear his official's robe at the execution, it'll be a dignified death, a death with 'face.' There are considerations for 'face' even in death."

"Which is why I think that you diplomats must let them save face in your dealings with the Chinese government."

"Yes, that makes a lot of sense. It's so good to chat with you. Too bad you're leaving."

"We'll get to see each other again. I'm sure you won't remain in Ningbo for long."

Chapter Two

The gunboat *Forrester No. 87* sailed past Fort Humen heading for nearby Guangzhou. In the gathering rainstorm Hart took shelter under an awning, but even so his trousers got soaking wet. It was almost the end of March but it was still unusually cold in subtropical Guangzhou. Hart did not have enough clothes on. He felt chilled and there seemed to be an army of tiny insects gnawing at his legs, which had been long wrapped tight by the wet trousers. But soon his attention was diverted from his discomfort. The gunboat was nearing Huangpu Harbor and he had no idea what would happen after he went ashore.

At six o'clock in the morning, December 28, 1857, the cannons of British and French warships had begun bombarding Guangzhou. By noon on December 29, Guangzhou was under the control of the allied Anglo-French forces. As soon as the news reached Ningbo, a transfer order arrived for Hart. In March 1858, he was appointed as Second Assistant at the British Consulate in Guangzhou, where the head of the ruling Allied Commission was Harry Parkes, British Consul at Guangzhou. This meant that Hart was to be a member of the Allied Commission governing Guangzhou, a radical change in status for him because Guangzhou was a huge city compared with Ningbo, with a population numbering in the hundreds of thousands.

Hart's thoughts had dwelled on Guangzhou for the entire duration of the journey. Unable to visualize what it would be like there, he had been feeling slightly uneasy. Now that Guangzhou was looming right in front of him, a mixture of anxiety and eagerness flowed through him.

At Huangpu Wharf, he transferred to a small steamer to go up the Pearl River to the city proper. His bulky pieces of baggage were to be delivered the next day by the public steamer the *Changsheng.*

Along both banks of the Pearl River were moored many crafts, mostly fishing boats. There were also lavishly decorated pleasure boats and ferries rowed by women with natural, unbound feet. On the pleasure boats lit by multicolored lanterns, gaudily dressed women appeared to have started greeting patrons. Life in this city seemed quite normal, with nothing particular out of the ordinary. But never having set foot in Guangzhou before, Hart was not yet ready to rate it against any other place he knew.

More than an hour later, the steamer pulled up to the wharf near Shamian. An English naval officer came to meet Hart, and led him ashore and into the city through the southeastern gate. In the gathering darkness, there were hardly any pedestrians in the streets and the stores were all closed. They passed Allied Street and South Street, stopping at the Commissioner's yamen. It was a palace-like building with a vermillion gate studded with gilded copper nails. Luxuriant tropical trees thrust their swaying branches over the tall fence wall.

The English soldier guarding the gate went in to announce the visitors. Soon an official, Administrative Assistant Arthur Rotch Hewlett of the British Consulate, came out to greet Hart. On their way into the Consulate, he told Hart that this used to be the residence of Ye Mingchen, the Qing Empire's Viceroy of Guangdong and Guangxi. After Ye was captured by the Allied Anglo-French forces and taken to Calcutta, the compound had become the yamen of the Allied Commission.

In Ningbo, Hart had seen some Chinese-style mansions with successions of three, four or even five courtyards, each surrounded by nearly ten rooms. A five-courtyard mansion therefore would have forty to fifty rooms. And each of such mansions also had a garden in the back. But none of those mansions was nearly as large as this one. Here, one courtyard led to another and one garden abutted another.

As they proceeded, Hart felt that he was in a labyrinth and had lost all his bearings. Finally they came to a small courtyard that was screened off a larger one by a small hill, which consisted of a strangely shaped rockery. They went around the hill and stopped at a medium-sized pond. An open long veranda led from the pond to a traditional "moon gate," which got its name from its shape. Pointing at the moon gate, Hewlett said, "Those are Mr. Parkes' quarters. You will be put up there." Then, pointing at a door that faced the pond, he continued, "You can wash up and take a rest there, and I'll come back to take you to see Commissioner Parkes."

It was a courtyard enveloped in moist green. Tropical plants of every variety, positioned in a charming arrangement, vied for space with their broad leaves. Hart thought that even a blazing sun could be largely blotted out here, and now he felt the onset of a chilling coldness.

Though it was a Chinese-style house, there was still a shower room adjacent to every bedchamber because of the need for frequent showers in subtropical Guangzhou. Hart took a cold shower in spite of the chilliness. By the time he had dried himself and changed into clean clothes, he felt warmer and the fatigue of the journey evaporated. As he was admiring the intricately-carved rosewood furniture in the room, Hewlett entered and took him to Parkes.

Parkes rose from the dining table to greet Hart, saying that he had been waiting for Hart to begin the meal. Realizing that he and the Commissioner were the only two people being served, Hart felt slightly flattered but uneasy. As he remained standing, looking awkward, Parkes said, "Come on, sit down!

Let's eat! You must be starving. I know I am." With that, he took up his knife and fork.

Hart produced a letter and said, "This is a letter that your wife asked me to deliver to you when I was in Hong Kong."

"Thank you!" Parkes took the letter and scanned it quickly while he said again, "Sit! And eat!"

Hart was indeed starving. He ate heartily and soon polished off everything. Parkes had a servant bring him Ceylon tea and a Havana cigar. "I've been looking forward to your arrival," said Parkes. "You need not go to the Consulate. Stay here instead, at the Allied Commission. We are swamped with work. I can't possibly manage all this by myself. You are going to be my secretary."

"What exactly are my duties?"

"I don't know what to tell you. I can't even describe clearly what it is that I do. Since we occupied Guangzhou our Allied Commission has become a government, but we don't want to be a government nor are we in a position to govern hundreds of thousands of Chinese with our one hundred British soldiers and thirty French soldiers. We're still trying to put together a Chinese police force of several hundred men. With what we've got, we'll be happy if we can manage to maintain order. Other things are beyond our ability. Viceroy Ye Mingchen refused to cooperate, so we had to pack him off to Calcutta. We hope that Bai Gui, Governor of Guangdong, will take over the functions of government but the Allied Commission also wants to keep him under our thumb. It's a difficult job."

Hart asked, "Don't you have two other Commissioners?"

"That's true—Colonel Holloway and Captain Martineau des Chavez. But they don't speak a word of Chinese, so how are they supposed to make deals with the Chinese? They only know how to make war. Acting Consul Winchester says you have an excellent command of Chinese."

"I can get by."

"He also had good things to say about your management skills."

"He may have overrated me."

"I desperately need people like you. Your job is to complete every task I give you, and to act on my behalf during my absence."

"In what capacity?"

"In every capacity possible!"

It was already eleven o'clock when Hart left Parkes to return to his own quarters. From force of habit, he opened his diary and jotted down a description of Parkes's appearance: "A man of the middle height: olive fair complexion, good features, light yellow hair, and soft, sandy whiskers. His forehead is significant of intellect; but his nose and mouth give one the idea of nervous activity rather than of determined character."[7]

His baggage still in the boat, he went to bed fully clothed. It was cold.

As he stayed wide awake behind his closed eyes, all kinds of thoughts came flooding into his mind. It looked like he had bright career prospects in Guangzhou but he had trouble visualizing the details of what could happen next. His thoughts went to Ayao. The order of transfer had come suddenly. Even though Hart had been looking forward to it, he didn't quite have the heart to take such an abrupt leave of Ayao and of Ningbo where he had been living for three years.

Ayao had known that Hart would leave Ningbo some day but she didn't want to talk about the future. Every time this subject had come up, she would say, "We don't have a future." Hart admired her for her rational mind. She was a strange woman, sometimes very feminine, sometimes very masculine, and sometimes both at the same time. After being told about Hart's transfer, she wept the whole night through but then very sensibly resigned herself to the situation. The next day she helped Hart pack, but during the night she abandoned herself to passionate love. During the day she was as level-headed as a man but after nightfall, she changed into a woman on fire. By turns, she transported him into raptures with the flames of her ardor, put him in a state of lazy stupor as if she were a tubful of soothing warm water, and then like a jar of rice wine, brought him into an intoxicated trance. Hart felt he might have used up all the joy that was allotted him for the entire span of his life. The next morning, he thought, tired and spent, that as far as carnal pleasures were concerned, he would have no regrets if he were to die this minute.

He still missed her. What a fine woman she was! He might not be able to find another woman as good in the future.

The previous night, Parkes had given Hart permission to rest for half a day. After breakfast, Hart wanted to go to the dock to see if his baggage had arrived. Upon reaching the gate he hesitated, but immediately felt shame for having had second thoughts. Being secretary to Parkes, the highest official here, he should be feared by the local residents, not the other way around. With one big stride he was out of the gate but a few steps further, it occurred to him that he was unarmed. He should be equipped with a pistol. But then again, even a pistol was useless to a solitary man. Plus, a pistol would mark him out even more easily as a target to attack. And yet, without a pistol he was no less of a target because his hair color betrayed his foreign origin. But he couldn't very well go back now. It couldn't be dangerous, could it? Otherwise the guard at the gate would have stopped him from venturing out.

He continued to walk ahead. There were pedestrians in the streets going in both directions. There were also loiterers who did not appear to be doing anything. The shops were open but did not seem to be engaged in business. When he passed by, everyone's eyes turned on him with blank looks that showed little emotion. Hart felt that all those eyes were fixed on his back, and a feeling of being pricked soon changed into shivers. Subconsciously he quickened his pace and headed straight for the dock.

All of a sudden a little boy cried out, "Wei loh [foreigner]!" He almost jumped. The adults standing by reproved the boy with their eyes but no one said a word. Silence resumed. Hart suddenly became aware of the acute stillness all around him. It was broad daylight and yet the entire street was just as noiseless as if it had been the middle of the night, the silence pierced only by the tapping of his leather shoes on the stone-slab pavement. Such an unusual daytime stillness frightened him, as if he had morphed into a ghost in a dream surrounded by other floating ghosts. He almost broke into a run. His footsteps grew louder and louder, jarring the ear like gunshots.

There was no *Changsheng* moored at dock nor did he see any other public steamers. Without a moment's delay, he turned back. By the time he was inside the compound, his back was covered in sweat. Once in his own room, he could still hear his heart pounding. This was an awful place, a city completely different from Ningbo. How was he going to make it here?

At noontime, Parkes sent a message to Hart, asking him to attend church service together at two o'clock that afternoon. It was then that he recalled it was a Sunday. The church was located in the foreign community's residential area outside the city proper. When his glance took in dozens of Westerners in the church, he had the feeling that he was back in the real world. Before the service began, Parkes introduced Hart to Colonel Holloway and Captain Martineau des Chavez, the other two members of the Allied Commission. Colonel Holloway was *a fine, quiet gentlemanly man*, while Captain Martineau des Chavez, on the other hand, was *cold and filled with hauteur*.[8] Luckily, the service began and put Hart at greater ease.

The service over, Parkes took Hart to see Bai Gui, the Qing government's Governor of Guangdong. His residence stood next to Ye Mingchen's former residence. Though it was not physically taken over by the Allied Forces, it was under their control. Bai Gui was thus under de facto house arrest, although his daily routine and his style of living remained the same.

Parkes had already said something to Hart about Bai Gui the previous night. He was an aristocrat of the Plain-Yellow Banner, one of the military divisions of the Manchu, the ethnic group that established the Qing Dynasty in 1644. Now looking at him in the flesh, Hart was deeply impressed by his towering figure and his imposing air.

After introducing Bai Gui to Hart, Parkes came straight to the point. Reproachfully, he said, "General, the current security situation in Guangzhou doesn't look good at all."

"I have the same view," said Bai Gui in a dignified but indifferent tone.

"As Governor of Guangzhou, you have the responsibility to maintain law and order in the city."

"But my immediate boss, Viceroy Ye Mingchen, is with you. I take orders from him."

"As far as we know, Ye is no longer Viceroy. Your imperial court has appointed a new Viceroy."

"Then I am at the command of the new Viceroy."

"But the new Viceroy is still on his way here. According to your rules, before the new Viceroy takes up his post, you must fulfill your responsibilities or be guilty of remission of duty."

"Being in a special position at this stage, I am simply unable to exercise my functions."

With a smile, Parkes said, "All right, General. I appreciate your integrity. You are a true soldier. We need not bandy words with each other. Let me tell you this: Our Minister is on his way to White River, Tianjin, to talk with your Imperial Envoy. We have no wish to aggravate the situation. We occupied Guangzhou as a last resort in order to push for talks so that trade relations between our two countries could advance. I believe the talks at White River will be fruitful. So leading up to that, we must not let the situation here deteriorate. Otherwise the responsibility of it all will be too much for you and me to bear."

Bai Gui replied after a moment of reflection, "Of course I

don't want the situation to deteriorate, either, but I …"

"I know what you mean. Why don't you assemble a contingent from the troops in southern China exclusively to maintain law and order? We can talk later about the troop strength. Also, armies of both sides must coordinate, to avoid new clashes."

"How do we go about the coordination, Mr. Parkes?"

"I will have Mr. Hart stay in touch with you."

The General's yamen at the foot of Bodhisattva Hill was richly adorned. On each side of the flight of steps stood a neat line of soldiers, French sailors on the left, British marines on the right. Members of the band of the 59th Regiment stood at one end of the terrace, their brass instruments in hand. *The reception room was hung round by flags of different countries, those of England and France behind the chairs on which the chief personages were to sit.*[9] British and French officers in full regalia, complete with medals on their chests, chatted lightheartedly in the room while waiting for their visitor, General Bai Gui.

The invitation for Bai Gui from Major General Van Straubenzee, Commander of the Hong Kong Garrison, and Commandant Supérieur d'Aboville of France, had been Hart's idea. After the visit with Bai Gui the other day, Hart had recalled his conversation with Martin on the city wall of Ningbo. Martin had said that the Chinese valued "face" above all else, a remark that had left a deep impression on him. Hart believed that in order to obtain Bai Gui's cooperation, it was necessary to give him "face." He believed if the highest commanders of the Allied Forces would issue him an invitation, this would doubtlessly be "face" of the highest order.

Hart, as the Chinese interpreter, had been waiting for Bai Gui by the curbside with the aides-de-camp of the British and French commanders-in-chief. At the appointed time, the distinguished guest's procession arrived. The General's penchant for pomp and ceremony exceeded Hart's expectation. The procession was preceded by a *man carrying a red umbrella;*

then some fifty attendants walking orderly two by two; then a man on a pony,[10] followed by eight yamen lictors who, for some obscure reason, were holding iron chains in their hands. Then came some twenty more attendants and finally the General's sedan chair carried by eight men.

When Bai Gui was seen alighting from his chair, Hart hastened with the two aides-de-camp to step forward and greet him. After the introductions were over, Bai Gui went up the steps with effort, his attendants supporting his heavy frame. A peal of artillery announced his arrival and the band struck up lively music. The officers in their glittering attire followed their two commanders and walked up to Bai Gui to shake his hand and bow in a show of proper decorum. With one bound, an army photographer went up to take daguerreotypes, a move that alarmed many of the Chinese because they had never seen a camera before. Bai Gui and his attendants viewed the bomb-like iron apparatus with suspicion but, doing justice to his title as General, Bai Gui did not forget his manners, and maintained necessary calm and dignity.

The conversation that took place inside was merely ceremonial and routine. On such occasions, there was no need for weighty words. The formalities themselves were imbued with substance. Bai Gui was evidently very pleased, as he had wanted "face" not for himself but for the imperial court and the emperor. In achieving this, he could now cooperate; otherwise he would have been guilty of a capital crime.

But the visit concluded in haste. At the same time the generals of the three countries were shaking their hands amicably, a Captain Bate of England was killed. To be accurate, Bate's corpse was found on a beach by the Southeastern Gate while the brass band was playing. The corpse had been stoned so badly that the army doctors concluded, after examination, that it was not possible to determine the exact cause of death.

The gruesome sight so enraged Parkes that impulsively he led a team of marines to "investigate." Hart, who had rushed to the scene upon hearing the news, also joined the team. In fact, "investigation" was just a euphemism for what they were set out to do. The soldiers led by Parkes surrounded the village nearest the spot where the corpse was found, and at gunpoint drove all the villagers out of their homes to the beach.

"Who did this?" asked Parkes.

There was no answer.

Parkes dragged out an old man. "Answer me! Who did it?" The old man shook his head, and Parkes dragged him to the edge of the beach. "If you don't tell, I'll make you die the way he did!"

The old man kept shaking his head. Parkes picked up a cobblestone and hurled it at the old man. It landed on his shoulder, causing him to cry out in pain.

"Speak!"

There was silence. And so another cobblestone flew over, this time hitting him on his forehead. The old man staggered. Blood flowed from his forehead.

"Speak!"

No response, and another stone flew. Another. And another.

The old man collapsed on the beach. Stones continued to fly, hitting him on different parts of his body, making different sounds.

Hart felt his heart clutched by one hand and his stomach churned by another. Feeling nauseated, he turned his face away but the heavy thuds of stones hitting the body kept falling on his ears.

Parkes went back to the crowd of villagers and said, "Did you see that? If you don't speak up, you'll all go the same way!"

Silence.

Parkes pulled out a five- or six-year-old boy. The boy broke out crying, piercing the silence. All the villagers cried out, "Let him go!" "Don't you touch him!" "Foreign devils!" "Bandits!" As they cried, they moved forward to take the boy back.

Parkes roared, "Back off or I'll open fire!"

His voice was drowned by the angry shouts of the villagers. The English soldiers pulled up the bolts of their rifles. As the rattling noise deadened the human voices, the villagers stopped shouting but did not recoil. With their chests against the muzzles of the rifles, silence returned. Both sides refused to budge. Some legs were shaking, as were some of the rifles.

All of a sudden, a gunshot was heard. Maybe the rifle discharged accidentally, maybe not. In any case, chaos followed as general gunfire broke out. Bare-handed villagers were of course no match for armed soldiers. Some fell to the ground while the rest backed off, but the soldiers continued to shoot. Maybe they were unable to stop immediately out of inertia. Blood flowed everywhere as the firing continued.

Hart stood immobile, in a daze. His mind was a blank.

Parkes called out to him, "Let's go!"

Mechanically he followed the soldiers on their way back.

Parkes said to him, "You've never been to a battlefield. It's always like this the first time."

The gate stood slightly ajar. Azhi, who had served as Hart's steward since Hart moved out of the Commissioner's home, was inside the gate, looking out. Hart now lived next door to the Commissioner's yamen. It was a small four-room bungalow next to the fence wall of Ye Mingchen's former residence. It had probably been once attached to the Ye residence.

One year younger than Hart, Azhi had been recommended to him by an English merchant. Azhi used to be employed by a foreign company but after the war began, the company's business shrank, and there was a surplus of hired hands. Having worked for three years in the company, Azhi had grown familiar with foreign ways, and he was a smart fellow too. Hart had tried him out for a few days and, finding him quite satisfactory, entrusted him with the care of his home.

Seeing Hart returning home, Azhi darted out the gate and said in a whisper, "There's a woman inside."

"A woman?" Hart said in surprise. "Who?"

"She said you know her. She said her name is Ayao."

"Ayao? Why is she here?"

Eagerly Hart pushed open the gate and went in. Upon his departure from Ningbo, he and Ayao had been ready to part for good. They had learned that England and France had declared war on China and that the Allied Forces now occupied Guangzhou, but they knew little about the exact situation there. Both understood that in wartime, matters of life and death and everything else about the future hung in the balance. Resigned to her fate, Ayao had said sadly, "I only had a predestined two-year bond with you. I had never even dreamed of being the wife of an Englishman. Well, we are not really husband and wife. It has just been a temporary thing, but as the Chinese say, 'Husband and wife for one night, lovers for a hundred days.' I will never forget you."

Hart said at the time that he would not forget her, but she had faded in his memory. On rare occasions, he had longed for women and for her but because his life was too hectic and unsettled, and because Ningbo was so far away, his unions of delight with Ayao seemed part of a previous life. Her sudden appearance now was like a dream come true.

Without taking the time to say a word, Hart pounced on her and their bodies instantly became one. Azhi discreetly closed the door after him.

After their passion had abated, Hart asked, "How did you get here?"

"On Captain Patridge's ship. It happened to be headed for Guangzhou."

"Where is he?"

"He didn't come. He asked a friend to escort me."

"Weren't you afraid of traveling to Guangzhou?"

"Aren't you here?"

Hart couldn't resist the urge to touch Ayao's soft and smooth skin. Watching her alluring contours, he again succumbed to desire.

It was after he calmed down for a second time that he began to tell her about his experience over the last two months. When he came to the bloodshed on the beach, Ayao said, "Stop! It makes me sick." And sure enough, she sat up and retched. Hart had not expected that a mere retelling of the event could cause such a strong physical reaction. He himself had felt disinclined to recall the brutal event, which took the lives of 57 civilians. While Captain Bate's death had been the cause of it all, the overwhelming majority of those civilians were innocent. He thought, "Had such indiscriminate killings of the innocent been unavoidable? Will I become conditioned to such brutality in the future? Oh, what a terrible thought!"

During mealtime, Ayao threw up again. Hart asked, "What's the matter? Are you ill?"

Ayao reddened and said, her head lowered, "I'm two months pregnant."

"What? You're pregnant?" Hart had not been prepared for this. His surprise was not accompanied by the joy of a father-to-be. His feelings were decidedly mixed.

After the beach incident, violence against foreigners continued unabated in and around Guangzhou. The killings were professionally done and left no trace. With these unsolvable cases on their hands, Parkes and the two other members of the Allied Commission got together to talk about what to do. They suspected that there were skilled organizers behind the scenes, most likely high-level Chinese officials who were still very much in the public eye. They had political experience and their words carried weight with the masses. However, they couldn't be arrested without evidence. In addition, the Allied Commission had never officially announced its takeover of the city. Without an administrative structure of its own, its governance must be carried out by the Chinese government officials. It was finally decided to put the leading officials under house arrest, cutting them off from the outside world so as to see if the violence against foreigners would subside.

On the afternoon of April 29, Major General Van Straubenzee and Parkes invited Acting Judge Cai, Guangdong Superintendent of Customs Heng Qi, and a local leader of the merchants, known as a howqua, to Bai Gui's office for a meeting.

Together they analyzed the current situation. The Chinese officials stated that in spite of some sporadic assassinations in Guangzhou, the overall situation in the city proper was stable and that the worst violence occurred in the surrounding counties. In Xinhui, for example, 1,500 "Braves," as local militia were called, had been rallied and were on their way to Hua County to join other forces.

Parkes asked, "Who has command over the insurgents?"

Judge Cai replied, "The local gentry. Guangdong has always been a prosperous region with no lack of scholars, and a good number of them have passed the civil service exams. Some officials are on leave in observation of the traditional three-year mourning period after their parents' passing, and their words carry great weight with the local populations."

Parkes said, "These counties are all under your jurisdiction. Why haven't you done anything about it?"

Heng Qi responded, "Our cooperation with you has greatly injured our reputation. Our words have lost their power to rally support from the people. They all see Viceroy Ye as a hero."

Parkes nodded. "You do have a point. It looks like the best way of giving you power and procuring respect is to make you appear as injured individuals in the eyes of the people. That can be easily done. Starting from this evening, you'll be confined here. Our soldiers will cordon off this house and announce that you are under arrest."

"What!" The Chinese officials were all dumbstruck. They had never expected such an outcome and were left momentarily tongue-tied.

"How can you do such a thing?" exclaimed Heng Qi.

"Don't get me wrong," said Parkes. "This is just for show.

Your food and living conditions here will be very good. The only inconvenience is that you can't go out unescorted."

Bai Gui said indignantly, "This is imprisonment! There will be grave consequences!"

"General, we are not going to impose restrictions on your freedom of movement. You can still conduct official business but, of course, we must provide armed guards to guarantee your safety."

"You call this 'freedom of movement'?"

"While you are here, you can talk about ways to put an end to the chaos. We only want to have the situation under control as soon as possible," said Parkes.

"Your approach will only make it get out of hand."

"Well, the decision has been made," noted the Major General. "Armed guards have already been placed all around the house."

After leaving Bai Gui's yamen, Hart went to the office of the Allied Commission and busied himself there for a while. It was dark when he got home. Azhi made him identify himself twice before opening the gate, explaining, "Two English officers have just been here. They looked everywhere. Luckily Miss Yao took refuge in a back apartment. They didn't see her."

"Didn't you tell them that this is my house?"

"I did, but they said they didn't care whose house this was. They said they had the right to inspect every house."

"Confound it!" cursed Hart as he entered his room.

Ayao had not recovered from her fright. She was pale and her eyes looked alarmed.

"Don't be afraid," said Hart, comforting her. "I'm here. It's all right."

For the last few days, Hart had been thinking about Ayao's pregnancy. He was somewhat apprehensive. Back when he was in Ningbo, he had been afraid that Ayao would get pregnant. His rational mind told him that his relationship with Ayao had no future, and he did not want to leave any problems to haunt them. He had discussed this with her and she had assured him that there was a kind of Chinese herb that could effectively prevent pregnancy. Indeed, nothing had happened throughout their two years of intimate relationship. Why was she suddenly pregnant now?

She said it had been two months, which meant that she had gotten pregnant just before his departure from Ningbo. In other words, this could have been a premeditated move on her part. She did not want an end to their relationship so she resorted to the most primitive, traditional, effective and reliable method to bind them together.

That thought disturbed Hart. He did not like being pushed around by a woman. He could not let a woman, a Chinese woman at that, to keep him under her thumb. It was not that he was not biased but he was a man of reason. This was why he did not discriminate against Chinese women but at the same time knew that a relationship with a Chinese woman could go nowhere. He was a diplomat, and a diplomat's wife was supposed to attend social functions. Ayao's looks and accomplishments might be good enough for her to gain recognition as a socialite, but she was Chinese, and from a humble background as well. It was out of the question for her to go into society as wife of a British diplomat.

The unexpected visit from the English officers helped Hart make up his mind: He must *cut the connection* with Ayao.[11] And this was the right moment.

After supper was over, Ayao quieted down. Hart's presence gave her peace of mind. She made a cup of coffee for him and took out some dried pumpkin seeds she had brought from Ningbo. Then she cracked one open, put it on her tongue, and fed it into Hart's mouth with the tip of her tongue. Hart recalled a folk rhyme that Ayao had chanted for him two years before, "Each passes over the tip of my tongue. The gift is small, it is the thought that counts. You need not have too much of a good thing. Forget me not, my love." Feeling a tug at his heartstrings, Hart couldn't help but gather her into his arms, feeling as if under the influence of wine. Parting with her was by no means easy!

Hart rose bright and early the next morning and went to Bai Gui's yamen. His eyelids were a little swollen because he had gone to sleep only just before dawn. One could not share a bed with Ayao and be serious about sleeping. It had been all right in Ningbo because he could easily dispose of what little official business there was during the day. But it was different here. His duties called for his undivided attention. He had to strain his mind to capacity to be able to iron out the difficulties.

The three Chinese officials were all in the reception room, each holding a cup of tea in silence, their faces betraying no emotion. Hart asked in the most gentle tone he could assume, "Your Excellencies, did you sleep well last night?"

"What do you suppose?" said Heng Qi angrily. "The sentries kept walking back and forth in front of my window all night, clicking their boots, demanding passwords and pulling their gun bolts, as if they were putting on a show of power."

Hart said, trying to placate him, "It was the same outside my house. There was never a quiet moment. But that can't be helped. To ensure safety, especially Your Excellencies' safety, one must be on guard."

"On guard against us giving you the slip, I suppose?" said Bai Gui.

"Oh no, General. We know that you would not leave this place. You'll be even less safe if you fall into the hands of the militia."

"Enough!" said Judge Cai. "Humiliate us no longer! Last night I was sorely tempted to cut my own throat."

Hart said in all sincerity, "Your Excellencies, I am just a humble secretary. My words carry no weight. But I think that our generals made this decision because they had no alternative. As I speak, representatives of the three countries are talking. No one knows what results the talks will yield, but until then, the three parties have the same task: to maintain order. And we also have a responsibility for your physical safety. Should anything untoward happen to you, we'd have a lot to answer for."

Since no objections were raised against what he had just said, Hart continued, "It may appear that you've lost face by being put under guard. I know that the Chinese put 'face' above all else. But in fact, in practical terms, your current situation gives you plenty of room to maneuver. You have nothing to lose but everything to gain. If you cooperate and keep the government functioning normally, you will have earned yourselves major credit if the tripartite peace talks succeed. If the talks fail and hostilities break out, we can guarantee your physical safety because personally we are on good terms. And, from the perspective of the imperial court, since you are under arrest and are heroes fighting us, how can any blame be laid on you?"

Heng Qi commented, "Mr. Hart, as young as you are, you certainly make a good politician."

Hart said, "Being only a secretary to the Commissioners, I am not in the game and not accountable for anything. It's a case of 'The spectator sees the game best.' If you have any specific demands, I'll ask Commissioner Parkes to come here this afternoon, so you can raise them to him. I can guarantee that you will have every convenience living and working here as in your own yamen."

With a nod, Heng Qi said, "Mr. Hart, Mr. Parkes is lucky to have a secretary as competent as you are."

But the house arrest of the officials did not alleviate the violence. Foreign soldiers continued to be abducted and shot by snipers, and retaliation against the Chinese remained extensive. Hart asked someone to rent a house in Macao, and had Azhi escort Ayao there. Left alone, he was struck by a sense of loss, but at the same time he also felt relieved. Now he could give undivided attention to his work. Because of his good standing with Bai Gui and Heng Qi, Parkes left dealings with Chinese officials to Hart. He had in fact become the secretary general of the government. Responsible for all matters of communication and coordination, big and small, Hart was up to his ears in work but not without the satisfaction of power.

Coordination was no easy job, mainly because Parkes lacked the magnanimity and flexibility of a statesman. He was too stubborn, and behind that stubbornness lurked the haughtiness and deep-rooted contempt for China that was common amongst many of the British and other Westerners. A little more respect for the Chinese would probably have prevented many violent incidents. Hart often regretted the fact that details such as tone of voice, wording and manners greatly aggravated the problems.

But there was nothing he could do as he watched the conflict escalate day by day. Hundreds of local militia assembled outside Guangzhou and fired rockets into the city, often breaching the city walls. Assassinations within the city were also on the rise. Police stations were bombed. Foreign officers bent on retaliation went on a rampage, burning down entire blocks of streets. Parkes was on a killing spree as head of a patrol team. Hart was also made part of the team. Pistol in hand, he followed Parkes in the role of avenging evil spirit. He worried about what to do if things went on like this.

Parkes had sent his wife to Macao to be out of harm's way, as Hart had sent Ayao. After delivering twenty dollars to Ayao on Hart's orders, Azhi brought back a letter in which she had copied a folk rhyme: "The green hills are here, the green water is here, but my sweet foe is not. Wind often comes, rain often comes, but his letters do not. Disasters don't hurt me, illnesses don't hurt, but lovesickness does. Spring goes away but my sorrow doesn't. The flowers bloom, only to add to my gloom. Drop by drop, my tears disappear, into the eastern sea."

Hart felt troubled. This woman was really in love.

Noticing Hart's darkened brow, Azhi said, "Master, in fact, folks in the city don't like the militia."

"Oh, why?"

"Those militiamen live far from here. They slip into the

city to kill and bomb houses, but the city folks get the worst of it. You should not take revenge on the city folks, or you will only drive them into joining the militia against you."

"You have a point."

"So you need not worry so much."

"It's not this I'm worried about."

"Then what's it about?"

"It's about her." Hart told the steward about his worries.

While Azhi was only a year younger than Hart, he already had two daughters and a son, and was much more worldly. Azhi burst out laughing. "What's there to worry about? To dump a woman is the easiest thing!"

Hart shook his head.

"If you pity her, give her some money. You are not married to her. Even if you were, you could easily have a divorce, as we do in China."

Hart kept shaking his head.

"Oh I get it," said Azhi. "You are not over her. You still like her and can't harden your heart against her."

Hart nodded. "That's right. She's a good girl."

"There are lots and lots of good girls. Her mistake is in taking this too seriously. You are looking for a woman, not a wife, but she wants to be your wife. She's got it wrong there!"

"Azhi, you're a wise man. What you said is quite true. But what's to be done?"

"It's up to you, Master. As long as you are determined never to see her again, I'll take care of everything."

"It's true that I am not over her, that I just can't harden my heart against her."

"Then there's nothing I can do." After reflecting for a moment or two, Azhi continued, "There is one thing to do."

"What? Say it!"

"Find another girl, one who is younger, prettier, lovelier than this Ayao. Of course, she should be told in advance that she's not going to be your wife. She's to be paid. Once you have a better girl, you can get over that Ayao."

This made some sense to Hart, and he asked, "Can you find me one?"

"Of course I can. You can take your pick until you find one to your liking. Just leave everything to me. Don't you worry, Master!"

"Do you mean to find someone from a pleasure boat?"

"That depends on what you prefer, Master. Non-prostitutes are also easy to find. Virgins, too. But you'd have to take the trouble of training such a girl. She'll surely know nothing and be no fun when she first starts out."

Unable to make up his mind on the spur of the moment, Hart asked, "What do you think?"

"If you want a wife, of course, it would have to be a virgin from a decent family, and then it would be worth spending time to train her. But if you're just looking for fun, to get over that girl, then I suggest picking one from those pleasure boats. Those girls are the prettiest and the most fun. They know their stuff in bed and they are trained in music, chess, calligraphy and painting."

"But isn't there the possibility of venereal disease?"

"If you really want a good girl, Master, leave everything to me—as long as you are willing to pay."

In the steaming hot summer of 1858, chaos engulfed Guangzhou. Acts of revenge and counter-actions kept escalating. Toward the end of July, thousands of militia launched an attack against Guangzhou. Although the attack failed, it aggravated the already tense situation. Hart was assigned a six-member team of guards to protect him whenever he left his house. He felt miserable and was pessimistic about the outcome of requiting hatred with hatred in a cycle of violence. Britain, France and China all lacked officials able to correctly assess the situation, make the right decisions and flexibly handle emergencies. Hart found his hands tied amid this sorry mess.

Upon returning from Macao, Azhi said that Ayao

demanded a parting settlement of 700 dollars, an amount that was way above Hart's means. But Azhi assured him the very fact that she had set a price was a good sign, indicating her willingness to let go of him. Hart thought otherwise. It was exactly because she knew he didn't have 700 dollars that she had made this demand, an indication that she was unwilling to let go. However Hart's mind was made up by now. He must cut the connection. In the months that he had worked as assistant to Parkes, he had come to see his own potential to be promoted steadily over so many mediocre officials, barring unforeseen incidents and interventions. He must not let a Chinese woman ruin his career, not even a worthy woman.

Ayao's worthiness became apparent only after comparisons. Azhi had found him two girls, both very pretty and charming but no match for Ayao. Ayao was his equal. This thought saddened Hart. He recalled a Chinese proverb: "Fish and the bear's paw, both delicacies, are not to be had at the same time." If you can't have both, you must not begrudge losing one.

Soon the year came to an end. After news about the signing of the Tianjin Treaty reached Guangzhou, the militia called off their operations. The security situation in the city improved significantly. The populace had become accustomed to the fait accompli of Bai Gui performing on stage as Parkes dictated his moves behind the scene. The imperial court in fact had also tacitly accepted the situation. They knew that Bai Gui was working for foreigners but refrained from removing him from office. Heng Qi was transferred to Beijing and promoted to be one of the six ministers managing the Zongli Yamen, or Foreign Office. As he departed from Guangzhou, carrying with him a good impression of Hart, little did Hart know the role Heng Qi was to play in his future meteoric rise.

December in Guangzhou was as warm as spring. Hart's work was not as busy and stressful as before. With the improvement in security, he could take walks on the streets, tour the flower markets and relax in the teahouses.

Guangzhou's dimsum breakfasts and soups were delicious. But he still felt slightly uneasy, even when he was having fun with women. After being paid 125 dollars in September, Ayao went to Macao and had not bothered him again. He thought she would come to demand the balance of the payment, but she did not. And nothing was heard from her for three months now. Was this a clean break? Was she still in Macao or had she returned to Ningbo? Hart became concerned. He couldn't bear the suspense and asked Azhi to go to Macao to find out how things were. Azhi said, "There's no need to. I know how things are with her."

"How do you know? Is she in Macao?"

"Of course she is. She was six months pregnant the last time you saw her. How would she dare to go back to Ningbo in a boat? If nothing bad happened, she should already have given birth."

"Given birth?"

"Yes, Given birth to your child."

"My child?" Realizing that his child by Ayao was already in this world, he had a sudden urge to see the baby. As soon as he obtained Ayao's address from Azhi, he set off for Macao.

She smiled. To his amazement, she smiled. She seemed to know that the man in front of her was her father. But of course she did not. She was not yet one month old, too small to recognize faces, but she was indeed smiling, her toy-like little hands happily waving, her little feet gleefully dancing in the air. Hart was enraptured. She was so sweet, his daughter. He was consumed with joy, a kind of joy previously unknown to him. It was not the kind that he derived from intimacy with women, or a successful career, much less from good food or entertainment. It was a joy that dissolved into his blood and filled the air. It was everywhere.

He gingerly reached out his hands and tried to pick her up, but her body was so soft that he felt as if he was trying to scoop up a pool of water. Helplessly he groped with his clumsy hands in a vain attempt to grasp her but only ended up making her cry. Instantly he withdrew his hands and looked at Ayao for help. With a smile, Ayao gently gathered the baby into her bosom. She lifted her clothes and offered the baby her breast. The baby immediately stopped crying and began sucking at it. Hart kept his eyes glued on the baby, fascinated by the way she greedily took in her mother's milk, looking adorable from every angle.

Having had her fill, the baby fell asleep in her mother's arms. Hart's eyes wandered to the fair-skinned, smooth, firm breasts that he knew well. As he impulsively reached out a hand to caress them, he said, "How can I bear to part with you?"

"I just knew that you didn't mean to break up with me."

"Why?"

"You are not a hard-hearted man."

"Maybe you misjudged my character."

"If so, I'd leave you without regrets."

Looking at her, Hart thought, "Maybe I really can't do without her."

Ayao said with a bewitching smile, "I love you. I can't bear to leave you but I won't attach myself to you forever. I know that's impossible. You are destined for great things. I won't stand in your way. When the time is right, I'll go away. I won't give you trouble. Don't worry."

Hart gathered her into his arms and said, "Even if you do, I won't let go of you."

Chapter Three

Returning to Shanghai after a seven-year absence, Hart found that the city had changed beyond recognition. A wooden bridge, the Wills Bridge, had been erected over the Wusong River. A street grid had basically been completed in the Foreign Concessions. The pavement on the Bund had been changed to granite chips, and most of the other streets had been paved with cobblestones bought from beyond the mouth of the Wusong River. Trees had been planted along the roads, a drainage system was now in place, and gas had been introduced for street lighting.

The names of the streets had also been standardized. Major thoroughfares running north and south were now named after Chinese provinces, and the east-west streets after Chinese cities. For example, Xiandao Road had become Jiujiang Road, named after the city of Jiujiang, while the former North Gate Road was now named after Guangdong Province. At street corners stood signs in both Chinese and English. Sidewalks were being laid out on Jiujiang Road and Guangdong Road to separate pedestrians from vehicle traffic.

It was March 1861. The roadside sycamore trees had just budded and the willows by the bank were tender green. Hart's mood was as animated as the season and this rejuvenated city.

He had been summoned to Shanghai on short notice by

Horatio Lay, Inspector-General of the Customs Service. Ayao and their daughter Anna, three years old by now, stayed behind in Guangzhou. He couldn't bear the thought of parting with them, but of course he also embraced the opportunity of a job in Shanghai. It was manna from heaven, something beyond his wildest imagination.

Lay, about to return to England on leave for treatment of his leg, had selected Hart and G. H. Fitzroy, Shanghai Commissioner of Customs, to jointly perform the duties of Inspector-General until his return. Hart had learned all the ins and outs of customs operations during his last two years as the Assistant Commissioner of Customs at Guangzhou. That qualification, plus his knowledge of the Chinese language and his experience dealing with Chinese officials, were the reasons why Lay had settled on him. It boggled the mind that a 26-year old was given the reins over the grand Chinese Imperial Customs Service.

Back in 1859 Lay had been appointed as the Inspector-General by He Guiqing, Viceroy of Liangjiang with jurisdiction over Jiangsu, Jiangxi and Anhui. The official confirmation of the appointment by the newly established Zongli Yamen had not come until two months ago, in January 1861. The letter of appointment, which also spelled out his functions, had been sent by mail to Shanghai on January 21 by Prince Gong through Heng Qi via the British Legation, along with a message inviting him to Beijing to provide advice on the Customs, trade and other diplomatic affairs.

Lay had received the letter of appointment on March 2. He thought nothing of it. To his mind, he had long been the Inspector-General. He firmly believed that the post of "I. G." had been conferred upon him not by the Chinese government that he despised, but by the British government. Two years earlier, as an employee of the Chinese Customs, he had acted as the interpreter and spokesman for the Anglo-French Allied Forces in the negotiations with the Chinese, making threats at every turn against the Chinese in his overbearing manner. He certainly had no other feeling than disdain for that "Zongli Yamen" thingamajig. Casually tossing the letter to Hart, he said, "You go in my place."

"How can I do that? You are invited by none other than Prince Gong, the Emperor's younger brother!"

"So what? I don't care if it was the Emperor himself!"

Hart was surprised that Lay had such contempt for the Chinese. He felt that Lay had abandoned a major opportunity, not only for himself, but also for Britain. The British had everything to gain and nothing to lose from a chance to exert influence on high-level Chinese decision-makers and advise them on the Customs, trade and diplomacy. But Hart let his words die on his lips because, as arrogant as Lay was, even if he accepted Prince Gong's invitation, little good would come of the visit. He might just as well save himself the trip. Hart went on to think that with such an attitude, Lay might not be able to hold on to his position as I. G. for long, because no government would entrust its Customs Service to someone so contemptuous of it.

"Maybe I'll get the chance that Lay is passing up," thought Hart.

Hart's premonitions turned out to be right, though he could not have foreseen to what extent Fate was to shower him with kindnesses in the next few years. These years were to lay the foundation for a career of a lifetime.

Lay's refusal to go to Beijing enraged Bruce, the British Minister.

In October 1860, the Anglo-French Allied Forces had attacked Beijing and burned down the imperial Summer Palace, Yuanmingyuan. Emperor Xianfeng fled to Chengde, leaving behind Prince Gong and Wen Xiang to deal with the foreigners. Already dealing with internal rebellions, the Qing government was unable to cope with an external conflict at the same time. On October 24, Prince Gong, in a nod to reality, met Lord Elgin, commander of the British Forces, to sign the Tianjin Treaty, which opened more Chinese ports along with other concessions. This was necessary in order to free up enough troops to counter the vigorous attacks of the Taiping Rebels.

Though he had a mandate from the Emperor, he did not have his trust. Prince Gong was in a precarious position. The Emperor could at any time easily charge him with high treason. He found himself walking on thin ice, always on guard against any mistake that could strengthen the hand of his detractors. Bruce understood his plight and didn't want the moderate Prince Gong to be replaced by a hardliner, which was why he had proposed inviting Lay, I. G. of the Chinese Customs, to offer expert advice. Lay's arrogance and brashness displeased Prince Gong and reflected badly on Bruce. So Bruce decided to replace Lay with Hart.

Hart was fortunate not only because Lay had voluntarily passed up the opportunity but mainly because of the timing of his ascent to the Chinese political stage. Prior to this point in time, the relationship between the British and Chinese had been highly tense, reaching its nadir with the burning of the Yuanmingyuan. However, driven by self interests on each side, the two countries had afterwards embarked on a path of cooperation. Hart's chance came at the onset of this stage. And unlike Lay, Wade and Parkes, he had been but an obscure low-level official during the hostilities between the two countries. He had no baggage. Finally, during his tenure as Parkes' secretary in Guangzhou, he had made a good impression on Chinese officials with his moderation, patience and understanding. Unencumbered, he made his debut on the stage and achieved instant fame.

The boat pulled up to Haihe Wharf but the passengers were not allowed to go ashore. The riverbank was thronged with armed guards, and it looked as though a search was on for some most wanted fugitives. Carrying wooden trunks and bamboo baskets, the passengers stood tightly packed at the cabin doors, making a great racket. Even veteran travelers grumbled that they had never seen such a thing. Hart was about to have Azhi find out what was going on when a minor officer led two soldiers down the gangway and, pushing aside the trunks and baskets, shouted, "Who's Mr. Hart? You are invited!"

Astonished, Azhi said, "Master, they're looking for you."

Hart was also caught by surprise. As he stood up to go, Azhi darted past him and called out at the top of his voice, "Make way for Mr. Hart!"

Hart was escorted by the guards to the wharf. A green curtained sedan chair was parked nearby. At the announcement that Hart was there, the curtain was drawn aside and out stepped an official in a red-tasseled hat that indicated exalted status. With his hands folded respectfully in front of his chest, he walked up to Hart in greeting. He was none other than Heng Qi, with whom Hart had gotten acquainted three years earlier in Guangzhou. Heng Qi had been the Superintendent of the Guangzhou Maritime Customs at the time, and had benefited from Hart's kindness when he was under house arrest by the Allied Forces. Later, through some mysterious connections leading all the way up to the Emperor, he was not only spared from punishment for the Guangzhou Incident but rose steadily up the official ladder until he was promoted to be a minister of the Zongli Yamen *cum* Governor of the Metropolitan Province of Zhili with jurisdiction over the important Beijing area. This was a powerful position. Surprised and touched that Heng Qi had come in person to greet him, Hart bowed in return of the courtesy and said, "What an honor for me, sir!"

"It's only right for me to come and greet an honored guest of Prince Gong's. And back in those days ... Well, this is a chance for me to play the host and show my gratitude to you."

Hart caught on to his meaning and hastened to say, "Let's not bring up the past. I know I won't."

Heng Qi replied with a chuckle, "Now please get in the sedan. Let's talk after we get home." He had rented a compound for Hart and furnished it with all the amenities of a home.

Hart said, "It looks like you want me to stay here permanently."

"Please do, as long as you find it useful."

After wine and food were served, Heng Qi waved off the attendants and said, offering Hart a toast, "I came here from Beijing expressly to see you."

"Oh! Is there something important that I should know?"

"Yes." Heng Qi rose, closed the door and continued, "Some things shouldn't be let on to a foreigner like you, but I am truly grateful to you for your kindnesses to me in Guangzhou."

"I didn't do anything, really. I did want to help you, but there was so little I could do."

"But you did help us a lot. You are the only Englishman who respects us."

"That's what any civilized person should do. I regret that some people who claim to be civilized are in fact totally lacking in that characteristic."

In a subdued voice, Heng Qi said, "I know you are on your way to Beijing to see Prince Gong, but I advise you not to go."

"What? Not to go? Why?" Hart was quite taken aback.

"Do you know that Prince Gong is the Emperor's younger brother?"

"Yes, I do."

"Do you know if they are on good terms with each other or not?"

"No, I don't."

"Well, they are not."

"Aren't they blood brothers?"

"Exactly because they are blood brothers."

"Didn't Prince Gong negotiate and sign the treaty on behalf of the Emperor? Surely he should have the Emperor's trust?"

"Well, someone had to clean up the mess."

"But why shouldn't I go to see him? He issued the invitation through our Minister. As far as we are concerned, he represents the Chinese government."

"I don't mean that you should never see him, but you can postpone this meeting with one excuse or another. For example, you have important business to attend to at the Tianjin Maritime Customs."

"I won't be able to stall like that for very long."

"It won't be long. Things may change."

"What will change?"

Raising his wine cup, Heng Qi said, "I'll have to stop here. I've already said too much. If you believe me, stay here and tell me what you need."

Hart also raised his wine cup. After draining it in one gulp, he said, "Thank you so much!"

Hart had planned on staying for a few days in Tianjin so as to take a look at the Customs House. But now, having heard what Heng Qi said, he was not so sure anymore. As an Acting Inspector-General of the Customs, he had no conceivable grounds on which to ignore or drag his feet on an invitation from Prince Gong, the chief minister in charge of customs affairs in the Zongli Yamen. And, Bruce, the British Minister, had also written to emphasize the importance of seeing Prince Gong. How could he not go?

Besides, he didn't really think that his friendship with Heng Qi was of a kind that would warrant a special trip to Tianjin for his benefit only. Heng Qi must have had an axe to grind. Was he afraid that Hart would tell tales about what he had done in Guangzhou? As Superintendent of the Guangzhou Customs, Heng Qi did indeed have an "itchy palm." Or, maybe he wanted to keep Hart under his control as a pawn in his fight for power? Anyway, Hart decided not to heed Heng Qi's advice. As soon as Heng Qi was gone, Hart had Azhi hire two horse-carriages and went to Beijing posthaste.

When they were drawing near Beijing, Azhi asked Hart, "Master, the driver wants to know if you would like to see Yuanmingyuan, the old Summer Palace."

Hart had long heard about Yuanmingyuan. A Frenchman who had been there had said, "Everyone who laid eyes on this palace, regardless of his educational background, his age or his way of thinking, was struck by the same impression: Nothing measured up to it. It was absolutely soul-shattering. To be exact, all the French royal castles put together could not equal this place." Yes, of course he would like to see it, even though it had already been burned down.

They were in a clump of ancient trees whose dense foliage blocked out the afternoon sun. A few more steps took them to an opening. Hart was instantly struck dumb by the vista. He had known about what had happened to the Summer Palace but had not been able to imagine what a burned-down palace would look like. He had never seen the inside of a palace before. He had no idea that a massive compound amid hills and water could stretch like a mountain range into the distance with no end in sight. The uniquely structured, elaborately adorned golden, green and ivory white buildings and belvederes lay in ruins. The broken glazed tiles and marble columns, blackened by smoke, were scattered among burned tree stumps and broken branches, looking unreal in the white sunlight of early summer. Only the quiet blue lake retained its beauty under the sun.

Hart could not for the life of him understand why the wise Lord Elgin, who had always opposed the opium trade, could have given the order to burn down the place.

Hart stood in the midst of what was past all belief to see, his mind a total blank.

Soon after leaving the ruins, he came within sight of the tall, thick gray city walls of Beijing. It was no easy task for even a 10,000-strong foreign expeditionary force with medium-sized canons and limited shells to destroy those walls and charge into the city. Moreover if the Chinese army had held on to their positions inside the city just to play for time and wait for the advent of winter, the expeditionary force would probably have withdrawn in the end. Hart could not figure out why the Chinese government had so easily opted out of military resistance.

Beijing was indeed a splendid city seen from where Hart was at that moment, with golden glazed tiles glittering in the sun and an Indian-style white stupa soaring into the sky. So this was the capital of China, renowned all over the world.

As he entered the city through Anding Gate, however, Hart was deeply disappointed by the dilapidation and filth that met his eyes. The streets were wide but not paved, and the gravel surface was uneven and sadly in disrepair. Passing carriage wheels raised clouds of dust. There were no sidewalks for pedestrians. The streets swarmed with people, carriages, horses, donkeys and camels, and were littered with garbage and heaps of dung. Sometimes he saw a water-well smack in the middle of the road. The pedestrians were in rags with vacant looks on their faces. He found everything depressing.

The British Legation was situated in Dongjiaomin Lane. The newly built white structure stood out from the surrounding gray houses succumbing to the ravages of time.

Upon the gatekeeper's announcement, Minister Bruce went to the reception room to welcome the young Robert Hart.

"What happened, Mr. Hart? You don't look well. You must be tired."

"No, Minister. It's nothing. It's just that I passed by the Yuanmingyuan ruins a few moments ago ..."

"Oh, you saw the old Summer Palace. Yes, it's very regrettable. Such a pity. But it just couldn't be helped. They captured our envoy, your former supervisor Mr. Parkes, and killed about ten of his attendants. It's a universal rule, and a Chinese rule, too, that two armies engaged in war do not kill the messengers. But they broke that rule. And they were the losers in that war, too. They had to be punished."

"I know. I just think that the Chinese will hate us."

"And be awed at the same time. Mr. Hart, this is war, a fight between two countries over their own interests."

"I'm worried that it will be difficult to deal with them in the future."

"No, on the contrary. But of course they will hate us. I heard that Prince Gong led a group of Chinese officials up a small hill in the suburbs of Beijing and witnessed the burning of Yuanmingyuan. Everyone present broke down in tears. At the signing of the Tianjin Treaty—oh how awe-inspiring we were! Our procession was led at the front by two military bands followed by more than a hundred of the Queen's Dragoon Guards in imposing uniform, more than fifty Sikh cavalrymen and two 500-strong infantry regiments. Then came more than a hundred officers, members of the general staff, and the highest commander. We sat in richly decorated sedan-chairs carried by sixteen Chinese men dressed in livery of the same crimson color as our uniform. The signing ceremony was held in the office of the Ministry of Rites. We were deliberately late by more than two hours. The entire process was full of the pride of the victors. When saying goodbye, I noticed that there was hatred in Prince Gong's eyes."

"That's exactly what I'm afraid of."

With a smile, Bruce said, "Young man, we are not dealing with individuals. Politics is about interests, not feelings. Faced with major threats from the Taiping Rebellion, the Chinese government was hard put to fight two wars at the same time—one external, one internal. So their choice was reconciliation with us. The same goes for us: We also had to make a choice, either the Chinese government or the Taiping rebels. The Taipings are Christians in name, but we believe that they are only using God as a front. What kind of a government they would form and what their foreign policy would be are all unknown to us. Relatively speaking, the incumbent government's policies are more predictable."

"But the Qing government doesn't seem to be of one mind."

"You're right. There are hawks and doves. The hawks are scholars good for nothing but empty talk, but they have the Emperor's ear. That's why we need the dovish Prince Gong, and the purpose of your trip is to help him and make him feel that we are genuinely behind him. You also need to inform him about international trade and modern tariff systems, and make specific proposals to him."

"I heard that Prince Gong is not on good terms with the Emperor."

"That's why we have to help him stand his ground in this power struggle. But how did you hear about this?"

"Heng Qi came to the Tianjin Wharf to meet me, and advised me not to come to Beijing. From the way he put it, it looks like there will be changes at the top."

"The Chinese Emperor fled to his summer residence in Jehol [Rehe] in June last year when we attacked Beijing. Then he became ill and has been getting worse. The latest news is that things don't look good. So there may be turbulence in the political situation. This is exactly why we must make the best use of time to push for British interests. We must not listen to Heng Qi. Some Chinese officials have nothing but their own interests at heart."

"When shall I go to see Prince Gong?"

"I'll make the arrangements. You can take a rest first. You may not be able to see him right away. Go to Wen Xiang first. He's the only Grand Councilor remaining in Beijing and is next only to Prince Gong in the newly established Zongli Yamen. He's a very smart and capable man. To a certain degree, he is more capable than Prince Gong. Prince Gong is too young and inexperienced."

Hart nodded while Bruce continued, "Of course, Prince Gong has the final say. So you must get to see him."

"I thought he had asked to see me!"

"That's due to our efforts, but it's still hard to say if

you will indeed get to see him. I believe the key will be the outcome of your talk with Wen Xiang. You will need a few days to prepare for the occasion, so as to produce a feasible and concrete proposal to help the Chinese government extricate itself from its plight. This stage of our work is of crucial importance. We must determine as soon as possible whether the current Chinese government is dependable or not and whether we can have its long-term cooperation. As an official representative of my government, I'm instructed to say that Britain will not be involved in a Chinese civil war. But your position as chief of the Chinese Customs puts you in a unique position. Theoretically, you work for the Chinese government. You are not a British official. You can say what I cannot."

"I see," said Hart.

What is now the renowned Beijing residence of Prince Gong had first been built back in the Ming Dynasty. It was later rebuilt to be the residence of the once powerful Grand Secretary He Shen during Emperor Qianlong's reign [1736 – 1796]. After it was given by imperial order to Prince Gong during Emperor Xianfeng's reign [1851 – 1862], it underwent renovation using plans designed by Prince Gong himself. Located on West Street north of Shichahai Lake, it was known throughout Beijing for its elegance and charm. Prince Gong had a multi-room verandahed hall built in the middle of the garden as a guesthouse and named it Anshan Hall.

It was here that Hart saw Yixin, also called Prince Gong, for the first time. It was June 1861.

Yixin was Emperor Daoguang's sixth son, and younger brother of Emperor Xianfeng. In September 1860 when the Anglo-French Allied Forces were almost at the city gate, Emperor Xianfeng fled north. Before departing, he had appointed Yixin as Special Imperial Envoy Plenipotentiary to take charge of peace talks. On January 20, 1861, the Zongli Yamen, or Foreign Office, was established on the proposal of Yixin, Gui Liang and Wen Xiang, with Yixin as its chief minister. The establishment of the Zongli Yamen marked the beginning of the Westernization Movement and, Prince Gong, naturally, became the well-deserved leader of the movement.

A few days earlier, Hart had already met with Wen Xiang and had a long, meaningful and congenial talk with him. That was why he had easily obtained the opportunity to meet with Prince Gong.

To Hart's surprise, June in northern China that year turned out to be much hotter than the "plum season" south of the Yangzi River. But it was not hot in the garden of Prince Gong's residence. As soon as Hart went through the Western-style white marble arched gateway, he became aware of a soothing and delicate fragrance. Once he stepped into Anshan Hall, he found the air even more pleasantly cool and refreshing. The fact that he was favorably disposed to this brother of the Emperor from the very beginning may have had something to do with the wonderful ambience of the prince's residence.

Prince Gong, in a graceful blue silk gown, looked more like a literary gentleman in a hermitage on a wooded hill than a powerful prince. Hart marveled at his youth and particularly the serenity of his expression. Hart had thought that China's plight in its internal and external affairs would have made the prince forget all about food and sleep in an endeavor to accomplish the task that had been so precipitously thrust upon him.

Sitting in a mahogany armchair, Hart could see, through the fan-shaped gateway, an intricate Taihu rockery. Later he learned that the rockery was called the "Rock of Dripping Green" and the cave under it the "Secret Cloud Cave." In the cave stood a stele that bore the character "fu [good fortune]" in the handwriting of Emperor Kangxi. But at the time, Hart was in no mood to admire the sights. He was focused on expressing himself in his still not very fluent Chinese.

He had come prepared. This was an opportunity not to be missed. He had brought with him nine reports with proposals to increase tax revenues to solve the Chinese government's financial crisis. To the current Qing Dynasty rulers, the Taiping Rebellion and the Nian Rebellion were worse military threats than the Western powers' invasion. The foreigners were seizing the opportunity to expand their influence on China's political scene by helping the Chinese government suppress the rebellions. Russia had proposed that the Zongli Yamen invite a small Russian fleet to bombard Taiping-occupied Nanjing. France indicated willingness to help the Qing court buy a naval fleet. On this last point, Hart had a proposal of his own.

"Your Highness, after comparing the Russian and the French proposals, I find the French one more reliable."

The Prince nursed his tea, waiting for Hart to go on.

"Dispatching a Russian fleet to bombard Nanjing shouldn't be allowed. It's detrimental to China's dignity, as well as unsafe, to allow a foreign fleet deep into China's territory and, on top of that, to provide them with necessary geographical and hydrological information."

"Right. Well said."

"The idea of purchasing a naval fleet deserves consideration. Bombing Nanjing from a vantage point on the Yangzi River will deal the Taipings a fatal blow. And the fleet can do more than deal with the Taipings. China is in dire need of a fleet for its maritime defense. If China has a naval fleet with enough mobility and firepower, no country will be able to easily land at Tianjin or other ports ever again to threaten the court with a force of just a few ten thousand men."

Hart was subtly making reference to the destruction of Yuanmingyuan by the Anglo-French forces, touching Prince Gong on a sore spot.

"I understand that a naval fleet is going to cost a lot," said Prince Gong.

"I have looked into the matter. Purchasing twelve warships of standard specifications costs less than one million taels of silver. The funds can be raised by increasing the opium duties and a sales tax. If you trust me, Your Highness, I will take care of the financing. The Ministry of Revenue need not do a thing."

"Oh?" Prince Gong had apparently never thought that such a good and easy solution would be possible. Subconsciously he began to suspect that there might be something else behind this proposal.

Hart had anticipated this. "This is a big decision, after all. You must consider it carefully, Your Highness. You can demand a French guarantee that the ships will be operated exclusively by ethnic Han and Manchu sailors and that the fleet belongs entirely to China."

Hart's plan won high praises from Prince Gong. It solved the problem of funding, was quite feasible, and ensured China's ownership of the fleet.

In the last few days of his stay in Beijing, a rapport developed between Hart and the high-level officials of the Zongli Yamen. Prince Gong invited him for tea on the terrace outside the "Green Seclusion," which was normally reserved for the prince's closest friends. The prince was making an exception for this foreigner. Embowered by verdant foliage, Hart, Prince Gong and Wen Xiang not only talked about politics but also exchanged anecdotes about foreign lands as well as Chinese and Western social customs. Prince Gong even lifted Hart's coat and studied with interest how a Western-style coat was made. After close examination, he said in admiration that the pockets were indeed "a great convenience."

Speaking directly, Prince Gong told British Consul Thomas Wade later on that he and Wen Xiang had the most favorable impression of Hart. He even went to the length of calling him "our Hart." To Hart, he also said in no uncertain terms, "The Chinese government looks on you as one of our own." Later, Prince Gong wrote in a memorandum to Emperor Xianfeng that even though Hart was a foreigner, he had a gentle disposition and spoke within the bounds of reason, adding that, since the post of Inspector General of the Customs carried a handsome salary, he would work hard for them to retain this post.

After assuming the duties of Acting Inspector General of the Chinese Maritime Customs that year at age 26, Robert Hart became the Inspector General two years later.

While Prince Gong was chatting pleasantly with him, the power struggle at the highest level in China reached a feverish pitch. Emperor Xianfeng had fallen seriously ill when he was still outside the Great Wall. When his life was hanging in the balance, rumors were that Xianfeng's younger brother Yixin, Prince Gong, was to replace him. Yixin's enemy Su Shun and his supporters turned the rumors to their advantage, telling the Emperor that Prince Gong was staging a rebellion. Prince Gong and Emperor Xianfeng had been ill disposed to each other in the first place and now, as was only to be expected, Prince Gong found himself in greater danger.

However Prince Gong was clever and politically astute. After Xianfeng passed away, he overcame great odds in a hostile environment, developing flexible strategies and making the most of his network of connections. With great political wisdom, he helped Cixi, the former imperial concubine to Xianfeng, mount a successful coup d'état, after which Yixin became Prince Regent *cum* Grand Councilor, a position inferior only to the now Empress Dowager Cixi herself.

But Hart was to learn all this only later. His experience with the Prince and his associates gave Hart profound insight into Chinese statesmen, meaning that he did not turn up his nose the way some arrogant and shallow foreigners did. While congratulating himself on having made the acquaintance of such a powerful man, he also admired the courage and wisdom of the young prince.

The role Hart would play in Chinese modern history was to be linked in an important way to Prince Gong.

Chapter Four

As the French vessel *Camboge* left Hong Kong's Victoria Harbor for Europe, the sea was lit by the fiery clouds of a gorgeous sunset. Standing on the deck, Hart felt that his heart was already in that distant country he called home. It had been twelve years! That young Irishman, the dejected college graduate who had planned on returning home as soon as he could afford a ticket, would never have guessed that in twelve years' time, he would be going back in glory as the Inspector General of the Chinese Imperial Maritime Customs.

He was understandably exhilarated that he was actually on his way to Britain for the first time in twelve years. But he also had official duties to perform on his home leave. He was taking an official Chinese delegation on a visit to Europe, the first of its kind in the history of the Qing Dynasty. The "Middle Kingdom" had been used to receiving salutations from foreign emissaries to Beijing but the Qing court had never dispatched official delegations abroad. And it had been by no means easy to come to this decision. Prince Gong and his colleagues in the Zongli Yamen knew the necessity of such mutual courtesy visits in modern diplomacy, but it had taken a great deal of work to convince the Emperor and members of the imperial court.

Hart's home leave rendered the plan feasible. With Hart accompanying the delegation, the Zongli Yamen felt that the mission was in good hands. In fact, the head of the delegation was none other than Bin Chun, Hart's secretary for Chinese correspondence. Having worked for Hart for several years, he had a smattering of English and was quite willing to go overseas to broaden his vision. However he had been no more than a county magistrate and, for the purpose of the visit, had to be promoted to the third-grade rank so as to match his status as an imperial envoy. Such a junior official with no diplomatic experience and only mediocre accomplishment, ability and moral character could hardly be considered up to the job. Hart must have had intense pressure to withstand.

But now it was homesickness that dominated his thoughts. He could not wait to see his elderly parents who were in declining health. And a young Irish woman was also waiting for him in that faraway land.

He had broken with Ayao.

It had been her idea. When the I. G.'s office was to be relocated to Beijing, Ayao refused to go. She said, "You are a high-ranking official now. You can't be with a woman like me. This much I know. Husband and wife must be well-matched in status. This is the way in China, and maybe in Britain, too?"

Hart did not answer.

"I'm not going to the capital where the Emperor is. I won't be able to show myself in society." She was truly an extraordinary woman.

In fact, as soon as he assumed the post of Inspector General, Hart knew that his time with Ayao reached an end. This had to happen sooner or later. As an important official of the Chinese empire, it was impossible for him to marry the daughter of a boatman. Officials at the Zongli Yamen were solicitous about his marriage prospects and some had played the matchmaker, but he had not made up his mind. Before he left China for his hometown, he had received from his aunt a letter in which was enclosed the photograph of a good-looking young lady. A British wife would indeed be a more desirable choice. After all, he was not planning to live in China for the rest of his life.

On the journey with him, apart from Bin Chun and his entourage, were his three children with Ayao—a girl and two boys. He intended to take them to England as his wards and put them in the care of a small businessman's family. He would be responsible for all expenses including their education.

Hart was a cautious man, a man of high social status with a sense of responsibility. While he wouldn't publicly claim them, he would not abandon his children born of a Chinese woman, as so many other Westerners in China did. He believed that an English education for the children was not only his responsibility but could also serve to put these reminders of his sin far away from him, on the other side of the ocean. Of course it might never have occurred to him that it was cruel to sever three half-Chinese children born and raised in China from their mother, and to let them live like orphans in an alien land, even if they could be assured of a decent living and a good education. The way he managed his personal affairs was with the approach of a politician and rigorous logic of a Customs director. This was perhaps what led to the misfortunes of his later family life.

However, to a 31-year-old man with a smooth-sailing career, worries were distant and unreal. In March and April of 1866, after passing Saigon, Singapore, Aden, Cairo and Marseille, Hart landed in Europe in high spirits.

Upon making arrangements for Bin Chun and his entourage, and seeing his parents, Hart went on to London. He had his fill of fun in that glamorous metropolis, which he had not visited in twelve years, having breakfast and dinner with friends, going to the opera, and associating with young women in the various clubs. Far richer and better informed than other men of his age, he was popular with the ladies, and he thoroughly enjoyed himself. He had probably hoped for love at first sight with a ravishing beauty but apparently he had no such luck. Returning to Ravarnet where his parents had moved, he stayed with them for a week before going to his hometown of Portadown to see Hessie Bredon, whose photograph his aunt had sent him.

In the charming afternoon sun, the foliage of the trees glistened as if with dew. The small town lay quietly in its tender greenery. The notes of a piano traveled through the leaves in the sparkling rays of the sun. It sounded like Chopin. Hart stopped in his tracks and listened for a while. As an ardent music lover, he seemed loath to pass by without paying respect to the music. Suddenly he realized that the piano notes were coming from Mrs. Bredon's house.

This was the town where he had lived in his childhood, and he knew the Bredons. Sadly, Dr. Bredon had passed away recently. Hart tiptoed up to that ordinary-looking two-story house. The shutters were open. The girl sitting at the piano by the window was none other than Hessie. He would likely have seen Hessie years before but he had no memory of her. What's more, as a Chinese saying goes, "a girl changes eighteen times before reaching womanhood." He had been afraid that she might not be as pretty as she looked in the photograph. To his surprise, she turned out to be even prettier, and compared with girls he had met in London, was more graceful, if not more beautiful. The joy in his heart seemed to be on the point of exploding like a balloon. He stood a while at the door, recovering himself, before he rang the bell. The music stopped. By the time Mrs. Bredon opened the door, Hessie had disappeared from the parlor.

Mrs. Bredon's "examination" did not last long. To all appearances, she was satisfied with this prospective son-in-law even though he would be taking her daughter to a distant land. To a family that had lost its male provider, the first priority was to find someone able to support the family.

Soon Hessie came to sit by an end table in the parlor. It was tea time. They spent a pleasant two hours together, talking about everything under the sun but always coming back to music, something both of them enjoyed. Hessie said that she liked Erard's piano, and it so happened that Hart had just bought a piano of that make to be shipped to China. It seemed that he had bought it expressly for her.

The subject of marriage came up on the fifth day. The decision to travel so far overseas was not easily made, but Hessie, Mrs. Bredon, and Hessie's oldest brother all agreed. Things went smoother than expected yet Hart remained uneasy, not because he was suspicious of the speed with which they had come to an agreement, but because he was debating with himself whether or not to tell Hessie about what he had done in China.

Of course he was thinking of what had happened between him and Ayao, and the three children! Maybe he should not tell, and yet he couldn't very well be totally silent on this. Otherwise should it somehow come to light later, his future home could be wrecked. But the truth was not something Mrs. Bredon with her traditional values could ever accept. Hart decided to write to Hessie. Compared with conversation, a letter allowed for the weighing of words so he would be much less likely to inadvertently give away telling details. Letters could also be kept over time and, in case of need, be produced to explain or testify to facts.

In the three months of his courtship prior to the wedding, Hart wrote Hessie eight letters, in the seventh of which he brought up his past. He wrote that in 1856 he had rushed into an engagement with an English girl in Ningbo but her father rejected him, a consulate employee without money and a future. So *the affair was knocked on the head*.[12] Then he prevaricated, saying that he had wallowed in Byronic "dissipation" in the following few years, ingeniously hiding Ayao and the three children in the word "dissipation." He went on to write, "My dear! I conceal nothing, but I make no unnecessary revelations!" What clever diplomatic language! He was leaving ample leeway for himself in case his youthful indiscretion should come to light later on.

Grateful to Hessie for her willingness to travel to a distant land with him, Hart tried to provide her with an English style of life. He could not move London to China but he could have an English house in Beijing. While in London, he bought a whole set of expensive English furniture and all the everyday articles that he could think of. In the following decades, almost everything he used in China came from England, except the air, water and fresh vegetables. A shopping list of his drawn up on June 10, 1875 contained the following:[13]

2 and a half cwt	*loaf sugar*
half cwt	*brown soap*
48 cakes	*scented soap*
4 lbs.	*ball blue*
1 dozen bottles	*mustard*
1 dozen bottles	*pepper*
10 pounds	*currants*
10 pounds	*raisins*
1 dozen tins	*raspberry jam*
1 dozen tins	*strawberry jam*
1 dozen tins	*marmalade*
1 dozen tins	*tapioca*
1 dozen tins	*sago*
1 dozen tins	*arrowroot*
1 dozen tins	*blacking*
2 dozen packages	*gelatine*
1 dozen bottles	*essences: vanilla, lemon, bitter almond, etc.*
4 dozen tins	*preserved herrings*
1 dozen tins	*parsnips*
2 dozen tins	*table salt*
3 dozen tins	*Abernethy biscuits*

6 hams weighing about 10 lbs. each
A chimney-sweep's apparatus

At the time he drew up this list, Hart already had a five-year-old daughter Evey and a one-year-old son Bruce by Hessie. He loved this family. He ordered a rabbit, a pigeon, a guinea fowl and a weeping monkey from England for his daughter's little zoo. He went to a great deal of trouble to buy a miniature violin and all sorts of toys for Evey. He demanded that clothes made for his wife and daughter must be "perfect."

But he lacked enough time and energy to be with his wife and children. His family crisis began that same year.

Chapter Five

When the gunfire started before dawn, the night fog was still hovering over the Daying River. Li Zhenguo smiled. He had seen this coming. Those foreign devils with their tricks! The day before, he had solemnly declared—as Alternate Regional Commander of the Qing Army stationed in Tengyue, Yunnan—that unless he received new official instructions from his superiors, he was not going to let the foreigners pass. Anticipating that the foreigners, by no means compliant, would sneak in under cover of night, he had deployed local militia in advance.

The gunfire would likely have come from the foreigners. The militia had very few guns. The foreigners were led by a British major with his upwards of one hundred Indian soldiers. But Commander Li felt secure in the knowledge that the terrain near Manyun was so treacherous that trespassing would not be possible without local guides. Taking a few guards with him, he headed for the river.

Before they had gone far, they heard battle cries that echoed throughout the valley. He broke into a run and, upon reaching the river, saw a crowd of people of the Dai ethnic minority, men and women, old and young, running toward the river valley and shouting. It looked like the British had enraged the Dai inhabitants with their gunshots, and the neighborhood had turned out en masse. Commander Li stopped in his tracks. He had not intended to make a big thing out of the situation; just to drive the foreigners away would have been enough. But judging from the way things had developed, everything had spiraled out of his control.

There were casualties on both sides in this conflict. On the British side, Augustus Raymond Margary, the interpreter, and several of his Chinese assistants were killed.

It was February 21, 1875. This was the "Margary Affair" or the "Yunnan Affair," which created a diplomatic crisis between China and Britain.

Hart received the telegram when he was practicing the violin. If it had not been a telegram from James Duncan Campbell, his London representative, no one would have dared interrupt his violin practice.

Wang Shun had been standing outside the door for quite a while. Even with the importance of the telegram, he dared not intrude before the piece came to an end. But of course the music had not come to an end when Wang Shun knocked and entered—how was he to know the right timing? Wang Shun was a groom, recruited three years earlier by Hart to be his personal attendant. Prior to that Wang Shun had done nothing but work for horse dealers, herding horses from north of the Great Wall to Beijing. He was illiterate. Apart from wind and percussion instruments at weddings and funerals in his home village, he had never heard music, not even famous Chinese works like "A Hundred Birds Paying Homage" and "Raindrops on Plantain Leaves." How could he be expected to tell apart Bach, Handel, Haydn and Vivaldi!

But it was exactly his ignorance that appealed to Hart. All that Hart wanted of him was to take good care of the horses, get them ready when needed, drive his horse-carriage, ride behind him to do his behest, and clean his desk and the floor until they shone. With such a personal attendant, Hart would have nothing to worry about whether he was writing or speaking in Chinese or in English. The man would not give away any secrets—not necessarily out of loyalty to Hart but because he was simply clueless.

But in the most basic matters, Wang Shun understood Hart, and communication was not a problem. For example, he knew he was not supposed to interrupt Hart in his violin practice.

The world abounds in music lovers but few are as devoted as Hart was. He practiced violin from seven to nine o'clock every morning, a routine never broken. This would be nothing out of the ordinary for a professional violin player or a teenager, but Hart was in his forties as well as being the Inspector General of the Chinese Imperial Customs. It is quite unusual that someone in his position would practice every day just for the love of music without material gains in mind.

With the violin tucked under his chin, the bow in his right hand, Hart opened the telegram with his left hand.

"From the India Office:

Chinese troops attacked a survey team at Manyun. ... On February 22, Margary and his five Chinese attendants were killed. The rest escaped. Three wounded. Luggage lost."

Hart put down the telegram, meaning to continue with his practice, but when his bow touched the strings, he could not recall what he had been playing. His mind was filled with the name Margary. To continue with the practice was out of the question for the rest of the day.

He went to Prince Gong's residence on horseback. Normally he rode a carriage when going out on business. A horse-carriage was a more appropriate mode of transportation for a civil official but it was too slow and he was in a hurry that day. What's more, he needed the jolts and the lurches of riding on horseback to work off his agitation.

He entered through the side gate on Willow Shade Street and went directly into the garden. He knew his way around the place. Prince Gong was usually in his quarters in the garden. The runners and guards all knew that this foreigner had a unique status. While admitting him into the grounds, they told him that the prince was away.

He then recalled that Prince Gong was still in a court session. He hesitated for a moment at the gate and decided not to go in. He and Prince Gong had been friends for many years now. Probably because Prince Gong was impressed with Hart, or because he was a foreigner, Prince Gong treated Hart with more courtesy than he did Chinese officials, and Hart was not as mindful of proper manners as Chinese officials were in Prince Gong's presence. Quite a few times, when Hart found Prince Gong away from home, he waited in the garden over a cup of tea, and no one would come to bother him. But this time, he hesitated. He needed to be extra cautious on this occasion. He left a message asking for an audience at the prince's convenience, and departed.

Turning his horse around, Hart headed for the British Legation on Dongjiaomin Lane. He was much more casual with Minister Thomas Wade. Though an official of the Qing imperial court, Hart retained his British citizenship, and being Inspector General of the Chinese Customs, he was very important to Britain when it came to protecting British interests in China. Therefore Hart was always received at the British Legation with extra grace and respect.

Willow Shade Street was not far from Dongjiaomin Lane, so before his horse could break into a decent trot, Hart had already come in sight of the British flag flapping in the wind. He suddenly reined in his horse and, after a fleeting moment of hesitation, yanked the reins toward the left and headed instead for Qianmen. He did not slow down until he was at Dashanlan, then he turned back to his own residence on Goulan Lane. Instinct told him that Margary's death would surely evolve into a diplomatic incident between China and Britain, and he would find himself in a delicate position. At such a moment, it would be inappropriate for him to visit the British Legation.

His official residence on Goulan Lane was a compound with

a succession of three courtyards. Around the first courtyard were the kitchen, the dining room and the servants' quarters. Around the second courtyard were the parlor, the study, the guest room and the music room, and around the third, his bedroom, his wife's room and the children's rooms. Between the second and the third sections of the compound was a spacious garden with date trees, locust trees, wisterias, and other flowers and plants. The rooms in the second and third sections had all been renovated with materials shipped from England. The fireplaces, lamps, mirrors, door locks and furniture were all from England, so when sitting in any one of these rooms, one could hardly tell if one was in China or not.

In his study, Hart again unfolded Campbell's telegram. He was probably the first person in China to have learned about this.

His first reaction was shock. He had known Margary. A friend who had been full of life and vigor only recently when they had met last was now dead and gone. He could not have remained indifferent, but Hart was not a man who would let his feelings run away with him. He was more worried about the impact this incident would have on Sino-British relations.

About six months earlier, in July 1874, the British Legation in China had made a request to the Zongli Yamen for visas for "three or four officials" who wished to enter China's Yunnan province from Burma for "tourist purposes." The British Minister Thomas Wade had sent Margary, Vice Consul of the British Legation in Shanghai, to serve as interpreter for the "survey team" led by Colonel Horace Browne. In fact this team was composed of sixteen "plant collectors" and their servants plus an armed escort team of seventeen Sikhs and 150 Burmese. They entered Yunnan from Bhamo along the Irrawaddy River [known as the Daying River in China]. All too clearly, this armed group did not square with the description of "three or four officials." The Chinese border guards were fully justified in denying entry to them.

Hart thought this must have been just an accident

because, to him, there was absolutely no reason for China and Britain to plunge into a conflict at this juncture. In the fifteen years since 1860, Sino-Anglo relations had been stabilized, with Hart playing a major role. Maintaining such a relationship was in the interests of both countries as well as being in his own interests. It would not do to let an accident break the decade-and-a-half long balance. However, in both Britain and China, there were always short-sighted people who hated to see a world at peace. It's often such people who make a mess of things.

Hart's worries were not uncalled for. Minister Wade was in a fit of rage, which Hart could fully understand. It was Wade's own assistant who had died, and it was Wade who had sent Margary to Yunnan. Wade gave a sharply delivered ultimatum to the Zongli Yamen, demanding a reply from the Chinese government in 48 hours. It was an impossible demand since the communication technology of the time did not allow the Chinese government to receive reports from Yunnan at such short notice. And to complicate matters, the internal political situation in China was in turbulence.

Not long before, on January 12, 1875, Emperor Tongzhi, son of the Empress Dowager Cixi, had died of illness and was succeeded on the throne by Emperor Guangxu, Cixi's nephew who was only four years old at the time. Then Emperor Tongzhi's widow Alute-shi, who had just been granted the title Empress Jiashun by the Empress Dowager, suddenly died at age nineteen. Her death was shrouded in mystery.

In the official version, the grief-stricken Empress committed suicide. But according to widespread rumors, the Empress Dowager Cixi had never liked Alute. Cixi, an opera fan, used to make Alute sit beside her when watching performances. During bawdy scenes, Alute would turn to face the wall and, much to Cixi's anger, would ignore Cixi's repeated demands that she turn back to watch. Responding to advice that she should not offend Cixi, she countered, "My position as empress is quite unassailable because I was greeted into the Forbidden City through the main gate by order of Heaven and Earth and the ancestors."

These words only added fuel to Cixi's anger. She took what Alute had said about being "greeted into the Forbidden City through the main gate" to be a veiled stab at her. Both common folk and the elite attributed Empress Jiashun's death to Empress Dowager Cixi. Commoners could relate to such cases of bad blood between mother-in-law and daughter-in-law, but politicians were concerned more with power struggles than with personal likes or dislikes. With Guangxu assuming the throne, Empress Jiashun should have been an empress dowager, but then where would Cixi have fit in?

However, by this time, Cixi had accumulated more than ten years of experience in government and had changed a great deal over the time since the death of the previous emperor, Xianfeng. No one dared make an issue of Jiashun's death. While the rumors did not lead to a regime crisis, the imperial court was still thrown slightly out of balance, which had an impact on the government's efficiency in handling diplomatic affairs.

Listening to Hart's explanations, Thomas Wade asked, "Are you sent by the Zongli Yamen?"

"No," said Hart. "This whole thing is not my business."

"Absolutely! This is indeed not your business. However hefty your salary from the Chinese Emperor, you are not supposed to do two jobs."

There was a great deal that lay behind Wade's remarks. The foreign staff members of the Customs were very highly paid. Commissioners working under Hart drew a salary of nearly 20,000 taels of silver per year. As Inspector-General, Hart was naturally much more highly paid. Foreign diplomats, including British ones, were green with envy.

There was another thing that had caused the estrangement between Hart and Wade. Back in 1874, the Chinese government had asked Hart to buy warships from

Armstrong Arsenal of England through his London agent Campbell, a project that Hart had been engaged in for a year. This was a part of Li Hongzhang's plan to build the Northern Fleet. Wade was not happy about the way, as he saw it, that Hart was overextending his reach. Later, in 1876 when the Zongli Yamen officially appointed Campbell as its warship-purchasing commissioner in England, Wade went to the Zongli Yamen to register his protest, citing multiple reasons.

Besides is it any surprise that Wade would look down at Hart? Wade was not only a diplomat but also a linguist who had graduated from Cambridge University when Hart was but two years old. In 1842 he was posted to China and became Assistant Chinese Secretary in 1846. A master of the Chinese language, he published his monograph *The Peking Syllabary* in 1859, laying a foundation for the system of romanizing Chinese (Wade-Giles) that would come to be named for him. In his eyes, Hart was a young upstart with little qualification to lecture him about politics.

The sky was heavily overcast. The freezing, howling, dusty wind of Beijing's early spring gave Hart chills even though his room was well heated.

The British government did not receive the Chinese government's reply in time and dispatched two warships to China in a saber-rattling move. Wade took his consulate staff with him to Shanghai, threatening to break off diplomatic relations with China. War was imminent.

Hart kept in touch with Campbell via telegrams to stay abreast of the latest developments. This was not something that fell within his mandate but it was significant to him. If a war broke out between China and Britain, what position was he to take? Would he be able to hold on to his post as the I. G. of the Chinese Customs? Was the well-functioning, incorrupt and highly efficient Customs Service that he had taken so much pain to build going to perish? He would never reconcile himself to such an outcome. He must come up with a way to avert a war.

What were the chances of his success? He had no idea. But he must try.

Finally, the Zongli Yamen approached him. Hart knew that they would, because in this situation, it was only right for him to offer his good offices in his well-acknowledged dual status. Though it was going to be a daunting challenge, Hart was still vaguely pleased. He could do something at last. And through this emergency, his importance to the Chinese political scene gained greater visibility.

The moment he entered East Tangzi Lane, a yamen runner met him to lead his horse. Everyone high and low in the Zongli Yamen knew that Mr. Hart was Prince Gong's favorite. None dared to be remiss in courtesy to him. Upon entering the second ceremonial gate, he saw that Wen Xiang was already sitting solemnly in the main hall. This veteran diplomat knew all too well Hart's importance in Sino-British relations.

Wen Xiang being an old friend of his, Hart went straight to the point, saying, "We must be careful about this matter; we can't afford to dismiss it lightly." Hart had said "we," honestly feeling he was on the side of the Chinese government. He told Wen Xiang that ministers of Western powers other than Britain had received orders from their respective governments not to abandon their posts without authorization. The German Minister Max von Brandt had already gone to Tianjin but had immediately returned to Beijing. He said that those governments had become aware of the gravity of the situation.

Wen Xiang asked him for news from England.

"I have learned that 55,000 British troops are in Rangoon awaiting further orders.

"Would Britain go to war over such a trifle?" Wen Xiang asked.

Hart shook his head, saying "The British government won't take it as a trifle. Thomas Wade sent Margary as an interpreter only after his application had been approved by the

Zongli Yamen. So Wade could take the killing of Margary as an act of deliberate provocation."

"But you must know that China could not have deliberately provoked the British."

Hart replied that he understood. "However," he continued, "it is more important to make the British government understand, to convince them there must be a reasonable explanation."

Wen Xiang promised that there would be one. "We will be conducting investigations. But Wade has now brought up a host of extraneous issues such as opening more trading ports, better treatment for foreign emissaries, exemption of the *lijin* tax[14] for foreign goods in the Concessions, and exemption of all domestic taxes for foreign goods shipped to the hinterland. These demands will be hard to satisfy."

As Hart listened, his heart gave a thump. When talking with Wade, he had been inwardly displeased that this veteran diplomat was so emotional. Now he realized that Wade was in fact not being swayed by his emotions. Hart had been too naïve. Wade had other things in mind. He was planning on making a big issue of the incident. The Margary Affair had all started with the British plan to open new routes from China, via Burma, to ports of the Indian Ocean. Since this idea did not work, the alternative was to open more ports on the Pacific Ocean. Wade was using the Margary Affair to gain advantages in another way.

"Could this be an opportunity for me?" Hart thought. "Can things that I haven't been able to accomplish be given a chance now as part of a package?"

A dual status had its conveniences as well as its downsides. In June and July of 1875, rumors circulating among British merchants in China said that the Chinese government was going to remove Hart from his office and appoint Chong Hou as the I. G. The rumor even spread to London. Hart did not believe one word of it because the Emperor had just authorized

Hart to purchase four warships from England, an indication that the Emperor trusted him, at least during the year-long period from placing the order to the actual delivery. He was confident that the Chinese Customs could not do without him at this stage.

As a high-level Chinese government official and a friend of Prince Gong and Wen Xiang, he believed in the Chinese government's sincerity in seeking a peaceful solution of the Margary Affair. The decision to buy warships from England, rather than Germany or France, before its problems with England were resolved, at least pointed to the absence of any plan on China's part to engage in hostilities with England.

In June, the imperial court appointed Li Hanzhang, Governor of Hankou and brother of Li Hongzhang, as the imperial envoy to Yunnan to investigate the incident. In August, the Chinese government decided to dispatch a six-member delegation to London to apologize to the British government for the Margary Affair. But it was no easy task to convince the British government of China's good faith.

Then in August, another incident, by no means insignificant, occurred, caused this time by a minor unforeseen event.

August 1875 was exceptionally hot in northern China. Even in Tianjin, a city not far from the Bohai Sea, the heat was oppressive. Two four-wheel horse-carriages rolled over the steamy stone pavement and stopped at the entrance to Li Hongzhang's official residence. Two foreigners stepped out—Thomas Wade, British Consul, and William Frederick Mayers, Chinese Secretary at the British Consulate. They were here for an appointment with Li Hongzhang to talk about the Margary Affair.

The gate of Li's official residence remained closed. Wade took out his pocket watch, glanced at it, and asked Mayers, "Is my watch too fast?"

Mayers replied, "No. Their watches are too slow."

Instantly Wade's face darkened. "That's hardly the reason. You stay here and get to the bottom of it. I'm leaving."

The gate opened just one moment after Wade had left. Li Hongzhang explained to Mayers over and over again that the gatekeeper had overslept because the heat kept him up all night. An appointment was immediately made for Li Hongzhang to visit Wade at his residence that very evening.

On the following day, a piece of sensational news found its way into English newspapers: Li Hongzhang had denied Thomas Wade admittance into his home.

In September and October, English newspapers were rife with stories about imminent hostilities with China. Campbell's letter of October 1 said that dispatches from China were alarming and public opinion in Britain was strongly hawkish, and that if these rumors were true, he believed China was at a critical juncture. Campbell's telegram three days later said that messages from China alternated between calls for war and calls for peace. If China turned down British demands, the British public was determined to go to war, and Wade never wavered from his hardline position. In November 1875, he was made Knight Commander of the Order of the Bath, a fact that spoke volumes of the British royalty's appreciation of his work.

Hart had been closely following the development of the situation, and was filled with worries. He must by all means come up with a way to prevent the relations between the two countries from slipping into the abyss of war. But his hands were tied. His influence on the British government was limited. However he was not prepared to give up. He believed he was the only lubricant that could move the two tightly locked gears. After many a sleepless night, he finally came up with a plan that was based on his understanding of the two nations: The British valued practical interests whereas the Chinese valued face. A face-saving compromise just might be acceptable to the Chinese.

He busied himself from October to January of the next year with drafting *Proposals for the Better Regulation of Commercial Relations*, which he submitted to the Zongli Yamen upon its completion. In it, he proposed opening the ports of

Chongqing, Yichang, Nanjing, Wuhu and Wenzhou as well as adjusting the taxation on a variety of commercial goods. This was written from the perspectives of the Chinese Customs as Chinese-initiated changes to the Chinese government's own policies. Even though these changes basically met multiple demands by Wade, they were approached from a different angle and, therefore, saved the Chinese government's face.

He was not sure to what degree the Chinese government would accept his proposals but as far as the Margary Affair was concerned, the Chinese government's position on its solution remained unchanged. On December 9, 1875, the *Peking Gazette* carried an imperial decree, announcing that due to the Margary Affair, military and administrative officials of Manyun were to be dismissed from office and tried by the imperial envoy. The same decree also authorized an increase of the annual customs budget from 748,200 taels of silver to 1,098,200 taels in a show of undiminished confidence in Hart.

Another good sign was that on February 4 when Prince Gong received New Year visits from the diplomatic missions, present at the occasion were about seventy officials of the empire of the highest levels, including all the Ministry Secretaries. The following week, all those eminent personages returned the courtesy calls to each and every foreign legation. This was a new practice on China's part, one that augured an improvement in future relations.

Almost at the same time, the British position softened. The Foreign Secretary, Lord Derby, said in an address to Parliament that Britain wished to maintain friendly relations with China. However, while Britain had no motivation to wage a costly war or do anything to harm its commercial interests, he stressed that Britain would not yield any ground in its demands. He also called on Chinese authorities not to shield those suspected of crime, whatever their status or official ranks.

The next few months were spent in waiting. The British

government established an investigation group with Wade in charge and T. G. Grosvenor, acting charge d'affaires, as the chief investigator on the ground. While anxiously awaiting the conclusions of Grosvenor's investigations, Hart saw some inauspicious signs. On May 12, he wrote to Campbell, saying, "Wade is now at the Yamen telling them his opinion of the judicial doings in Yunnan. He is eminently dissatisfied, and will give us all sorts of anxiety for weeks to come. He does not yet know what he'll demand; but what he is in search of is that *ignis fatuus*; a something that shall guarantee the future! … Wen Hsiang is still on sick leave and is either very ill, or is shamming to keep out of the scrimmage."

Wen Xiang had been a Grand Councilor and a Zongli Yamen minister for many years. His political savvy and diplomatic experience were unequalled in the imperial court. But he was indeed gravely ill, and died soon thereafter. The very fact that Hart had suspected him of shamming goes to show that the Chinese government's problem might prove well nigh impossible to solve.

It was also a thorny problem for Hart. He was in the same awkward position as a man hopelessly trying to mediate between his wife and his mother. Hart's understanding of both countries reduced him to despair.

On June 16, Sino-British negotiations on the Margary Affair broke down, with Wade threatening military force and a severance of diplomatic relations. For the third time he left Beijing and went to Shanghai.

The days from the last week of June to the end of August were a difficult time for Hart. He had to make a tough choice—in fact, a political gamble. In the negotiations, he had to take a stand.

During this period, Hart's mind kept going back to his predecessor Horatio Lay, and an incident that had happened years ago.

While Lay had been the first Inspector General of the Chinese Customs, he had proven to be a brash and insolent man who put himself above even the Chinese Emperor. He had said, "My position was that of a foreigner engaged by the Chinese government to perform certain work for them, not *under* them. I need scarcely observe in passing that the notion of a gentleman serving under an Asiatic barbarian is preposterous."[15] Being the I. G. he fancied himself to be a leading figure of the Chinese imperial government. This was the attitude that had directly led to the Lay-Osborn Flotilla Incident of 1862.

In 1861, the Chinese government had asked Lay to act on its behalf and purchase a naval flotilla from England because he happened to be on leave in England at the time. Calling himself "the first Lord of the Admiralty" in China in his own overblown estimation, he not only bought warships but also recruited sailors in London. He went on to openly appoint Sherard Osborn, one of his recruits, as commander of the flotilla, in an attempt to usurp power so that he could direct the fleet.

In May 1862, when Lay returned to Beijing, he went to see Li Hongzhang to discuss financial questions with Li in his capacity as the I. G. During the conversation, Lay casually let slip something about more than 600 British naval officers and men about to come to China on eight gunboats. Li Hongzhang was shocked at this discrepancy with Hart's proposal, and after Lay was gone, he rushed to the Zongli Yamen to put Prince Gong and Wen Xiang on alert.

Sure enough, in June, Lay produced a contract that he had signed with Captain Osborn, according to which Osborn would obey the Qing Emperor's orders only when they were directly issued to Lay. As intermediary, Lay could refuse to transmit the orders if he was not satisfied with them. On top of that, Lay demanded that as I. G., he must personally control disposal of the Customs revenues and the funds for the new flotilla as well as for all Chinese troops being trained by foreigners.[16] If these conditions were not met, he threatened to pull all foreign staff out of the Chinese Customs. In his high and mighty manner, he also demanded to have Prince Su's residence as his living quarters. He even went so far as to say, "The Chinese will do nothing except under coercion."[17]

Lay's overbearing manner antagonized the Qing authorities. Even Minister Bruce felt himself in a bind. Prince Gong wrote an angry missive to the Throne, saying that this exceptionally crafty foreigner was notorious among both Chinese and foreigners, and that after repeated failed attempts to dismiss him from office, this was a good opportunity to do so.

Lay also put Hart on the spot. The purchase of a naval flotilla had been Hart's proposal to Prince Gong, but Hart had clearly stated that the flotilla was to be under Chinese command, which was why Hart had won the trust and good graces of Prince Gong. Lay's actions were in direct contravention of Hart's intentions. It would have been a serious matter if the Chinese government had suspected Hart of working in collusion with Lay. But Lay was Hart's immediate boss, and he could hardly contradict him outright.

Resignedly, Hart made a compromise proposal: Osborn was to be an "assistant commander" under a Chinese naval commander to be appointed by Zeng Guofan. Both commanders were to be subject to the authority of Zeng Guofan and Li Hongzhang. In fact, this proposal saved only a fraction of face for China. The actual command of the flotilla would still be in Osborn's hands. Zeng and Li both worried that it would be too hard to control the 600 English sailors. However, the Chinese government was afraid of hurting Sino-British relations at a moment when the political situation in the imperial court was volatile. So, since it did not lose face too badly, it accepted the proposal.

However upon his arrival with the flotilla in September, Osborn complained bitterly about being nothing more than an assistant commander. On October 18, encouraged by Lay, Osborn issued an ultimatum to the Zongli Yamen: Either they confirm his agreement with Lay within 48 hours or he would immediately disband the force. The Zongli Yamen firmly turned him down. Finally, under the mediation of the American Minister, a compromise was reached. The force was to be repatriated to England in the flotilla vessels and the vessels were to be sold there. The Zongli Yamen accorded Osborn and Lay each a financial settlement by way of compensation.

At the same time, however, Lay was dismissed and officially replaced by Hart. The event that had put Hart in an awkward position ended surprisingly with Hart's promotion. Though delighted, he also filed away in his memory the lesson that Lay's failure had driven home to him.

Following this incident, Lay had gone back to England. No longer the I. G. of the Chinese Customs, he never amounted to anything thereafter. A series of ill-advised investments exhausted his means, to a point where he had to repeatedly borrow money from Hart in order to maintain a decent living. Hart was aware that what had happened to Lay could also happen to him in the future. Should he ever lose the Chinese government's trust and be dismissed from office, he might very well go the way of Horatio Nelson Lay.

The rattle of wheels on the stone pavement of the Bund grated on Hart's nerves. He was in Shanghai to offer his good offices at the behest of the imperial court, and he had high hopes for the success of his mediation efforts.

This was not the first time he played the mediator between China and Britain. He was again reminded of an incident from many years earlier. At the end of summer of 1862, Li Hongzhang's Huai army and Gordon's Ever-Victorious Army had jointly launched attacks against Taiping-controlled Suzhou. As their offensive stalled, they changed tactics and tried to induce the Taipings to surrender.

The rebel Tan Shaoguang, who had proclaimed himself King Mu, was in charge of defense of the city, and he firmly rejected any overtures. However his subordinate Gao Yongkuan, King Na, assassinated him and surrendered on December 4. While secretly negotiating with King Na,

Gordon had promised to spare his life. Yet two days after the surrender, Li executed him. Gordon was enraged that his promise to King Na had been broken by Li. Threatening to resign, he returned in a huff to his base in Kunshan, even saying that he would help the Taiping rebels take back Suzhou. In mortification, the Zongli Yamen asked Hart to go to Suzhou and Kunshan to mediate.

Li Hongzhang, for his part, was mystified. What was all the fuss about? He explained that he had ordered the execution of King Na because he felt the surrendering men were most likely only pretending to surrender, as other Taiping rebels had done. They had not shaved their foreheads [which was, for a man, a sign of rebellion] nor shed their uniforms. Li also stressed the danger of keeping the more than 10,000 surrendered soldiers in Suzhou under their commander.

But his explanations were not enough to convince the Westerners. The foreign community in China and some diplomats also reacted strongly to the killing of the surrendered. Hart was deeply aware of the challenges in his mission but he decided not to rush things. En route to Suzhou he even found time to go on a hunting trip because he was confident that, since assisting the Chinese government in suppressing the Taiping Rebellion was an established policy of the British government, the British Minister would surely exert pressure on Gordon, and Gordon would not go against orders.

However, unlike that situation with Gordon more than ten years earlier, Hart was now facing not the chief of a mercenary army but Thomas Wade, British Minister, an official representative of the government of Hart's motherland!

On July 4, still plagued by anxiety, Hart received a telegram from Campbell, informing him about the eruption of the Serbian-Ottoman War. He began to hope that, by a stroke of luck, England would be tied down by the war in Europe and would therefore have little energy to make trouble for China. On July 15, he sent Campbell a telegram as soon as he arrived in Shanghai asking him about the European situation, since

Chinese affairs would depend on it. Was a major war possible? Who was likely to help whom? Would the British Foreign Office settle for an indemnity and a peaceful solution or was it going to wage a war on China? He wanted an immediate response, but Campbell's reply, when it came, was that there was little possibility of a war involving all of Europe. Campbell remained silent on the British government's attitude toward China.

With good luck unlikely to materialize, Hart had no alternative but to take a more realistic way out. He pinned his hopes on Wade, meaning to talk him around so as to avert any extreme outcomes.

His four-wheel horse-carriage turned a corner and drove into the British Consulate, housed in a Victorian mansion on the southern bank of Suzhou Creek. Even though it was the height of summer in Shanghai, it was still quite comfortable sitting on the spacious veranda facing the lawn, enjoying the breezes from the Huangpu River. The Ceylon tea with lemon was quite palatable. Had the topic of conversation been different, it would have been a most pleasant afternoon.

"Mr. Minister, I am talking to you not in my capacity as the I. G. of the Qing Empire but as a British subject. Believe me, I'm on the side of Britain. For the sake of British interest, we need to maintain friendly relations with China. Otherwise other countries will come to 'plunder a burning house.'"

The Minister interrupted Hart. "You can't be completely on the British side since you have another identity: the I. G. of the Chinese Customs."

The same thing had been said to Hart before by another man. Guo Songtao, the first Chinese ambassador to England, had recorded the following conversation with Hart in his *Journals in London and Paris*:

"In your own estimation, are you on the side of Britain or China?"

"I don't lean to either side. Take horse-riding for example.

If you lean to one side, you won't be able to keep your seat. So I mediate between the two sides."

"When everything goes well, you can remain neutral. But what if you can't remain neutral when something happens?"

Replying with a smile, Hart said, "I am a British subject."

Hart was being truthful when he said this to the Chinese ambassador, but he was not being truthful with the British Minister on this occasion.

Hart nodded and said to Wade, "Yes, I am the I. G. of the Chinese Customs. If a war breaks out between the two countries, I'll most likely lose my post as the I. G. So I wish for the success of the negotiations. But my position as the I. G. does not serve *my* interests only. Would you wish to have a German or a Russian to replace me?"

"No, of course not," said the Minister. "But your post must not be kept at the expense of British honor and the larger interests."

Hart knew that this minister was not an easy person to deal with. He must be prepared for the worst. If relations between the two countries were heading for doom because of this Mr. Wade's obstinacy, what was he to do?

Hart suffered from insomnia almost every night during the two months he spent in Shanghai, from July to August 1876. The choice between China and Britain, and between reason and emotions, was a tough one. Again and again he paid visits to Wade, hoping to soften his stand on China, but each time their talk ended in bitterness. There being no middle-of-the-road option for him, Hart decided to stand firmly on China's side in this diplomatic crisis.

Autumn was already in the August air in Yantai, a coastal city between Beijing and Shanghai. Breezes from the sea through the large open windows shook the scroll on the wall, the work of the ancient master calligrapher Huang Tingjian [1045 – 1105], making a clattering sound. Thomas Wade sat stiffly in the mahogany armchair, his face dark and drawn. He had come here unwillingly from Shanghai, at Hart's insistence. His look of reluctance was primarily for show, a gesture like his self-imposed stay in far-away Shanghai. In fact, as the British Minister, he could not refuse to talk with the Chinese government.

Li Hongzhang, Minister of the Three Trading Ports (beiyang dachen), was all smiles. He was the court-appointed special envoy mandated to negotiate with Wade on the Margary Affair. Prior to his departure from Beijing, Prince Gong had broken his own rule and invited Li to a feast at his home. Needless to say, this was, as Li understood it, a farewell feast sending him off to the battlefield. In order to yield less on substantial matters, there was nothing for it but to lose some ground as far as face was concerned.

Hart was Li's assistant in the talks. He had no idea how the negotiations would turn out. He had been in touch with the British government through Campbell, to keep up to speed with the British government's attitude and the Burmese situation. It looked like the British government's attitude depended directly on Wade's attitude. Wade, after all, was Britain's official diplomatic representative.

The negotiations focused on what to do with Cen Yuying, who had already been dismissed as Governor of Yunnan. Wade demanded that Cen and other officials and members of the local gentry be summoned to Beijing for interrogation. Li replied that only when sufficient evidence was produced to substantiate the charges against Cen could they be sent under guard to Beijing. Unsubstantiated charges based only on suspicions would not justify such a procedure. The Chinese government had no reason not to believe the last report of the imperial envoy who had made a special trip to Yunnan to investigate the matter. Li Hongzhang asked that Wade present in writing his accusations and any evidence against Governor Cen.

After the session was over, the interpreter of the British Legation asked to see Li. The interpreter noted that preparation of written documents was very time-consuming, and then hinted that if the Empress Dowager would agree to a private audience with the British Minister, the accusations against the former Viceroy could be withdrawn.

It was all too clear that Wade had no evidence and could produce no written documents. Judging from the interpreter's wording, the British terms of negotiation were frivolous, impulsive, and disorganized. Hart felt that Wade's extremist attitude was highly dangerous and was very likely to take the two countries to the brink of war.

Hart sent Campbell a telegram asking him to think of a way to urge the British government to send a special mission in replacement of Wade. At the same time, feeling that the British government had put itself in Wade's hands because it knew too little about China, Hart drafted some wire dispatches under a pseudonym, objectively reporting on the situation. He asked Campbell to find a way to have these dispatches published in British newspapers so as to have public opinion exert influence on the political establishment.

It was quite a romantic notion, and Campbell immediately sent a reply from London saying that it was an impossible task. He said that worries about a Sino-British war and the preparations for it were only a concern for Chinese newspapers. The British press, in general, was ignorant, unconcerned and silent about the Chinese situation. They were totally engrossed in the issue of the Ottoman Empire, where violence had erupted, and Russia, which was seizing the situation for its own expansionist purposes. This was happening at Europe's doorstep and, of course, demanded more attention from Britain.

However, Hart took a long-term perspective. In order to supply the Western public with reliable accounts of affairs in China and elsewhere in the Far East, Hart took counsel with Campbell and came up with the idea of a Chinese Customs-funded London publication on the Far East. Campbell called on Dr. William Howard Russell, a correspondent for *The*

Times, whose son was an employee of the Chinese Customs. Russell recommended purchasing a weekly newspaper that was for sale, *The United States Gazette*, and, with himself as the editor, gradually transforming it into an authoritative outlet for Far Eastern news—concealing from the public, however, the fact of its Chinese government ownership.[18] With 2,000 pounds, Campbell bought the weekly but, after failing to make a success of it, sold it in 1878.

In the course of the Yantai (Chefoo) negotiations, an aide to Li Hongzhang discovered that some things discussed confidentially had come into the knowledge of a secretary of the British Legation. The number-one suspect of the leakage was Li Hongzhang's son-in-law, son of a cabinet minister. Not knowing what to do, the aide sought Hart's opinion.

That very evening when he was alone with Li, Hart asked, "Sir, do you have a gunboat here?"

"Yes," replied Li.

"Can you order the gunboat to prepare for sailing at dawn tomorrow, sir?"

"Yes, of course, if necessary. Why do you ask?"

"I'd like to have it send a letter for me to Tianjin."

"A letter to whom?"

"The letter is not important. The courier carrying it is."

As smart as he was, Li instantly caught on. "Who is he? If any of my men dares betray me, I'll have him done away with."

"When you were in Tianjin, McPherson delivered an oral message from me to you. Present on that occasion were you, McPherson and another person. The contents of that message came to the knowledge of the British Consulate three days later." Well aware of who that "other person" was, Li vowed, "I'll take care of this."

The negotiations finally yielded an outcome. On September 12, Li and Wade formally signed an agreement that was favorable to Britain, calling for a payment of 200,000 taels of silver from

China to the bereaved family and an apology mission from China to Britain. There was to be a British investigation mission from India stationed in Yunnan for five years to observe the conditions of trade in order to develop trade regulations. The agreement also expanded consular jurisdiction, and whenever a crime affected the person or property of a British subject, whether in the interior or at the open ports, the case was to be tried by officials of the defendant's nationality.

Britain's advantages through the agreement also included the opening of four new ports—Yichang, Wuhu, Wenzhou and Beihai—and steamers allowed for the purpose of landing or shipping passengers or goods on another six places. It exempted the *lijin* tax on foreign goods in Concessions of the treaty ports and outlawed other forms of taxes on foreign goods except inland transit dues. Finally, a British mission of exploration was permitted from Beijing through Gansu, Qinghai or Sichuan to Tibet, and thence to India, or across the Indian frontier to Tibet.

Wade also made some compromises, however he advanced three steps before taking one step back, and secured significant trade benefits for Britain.

Of course with the contrast between China and Britain in terms of power, any negotiation could end only in concessions on China's part. This was beyond anyone's individual will. While the talks were going on, a British naval fleet consisting of four well-armed cruisers was anchored in Dalian Bay facing Yantai, where the negotiations took place. It is not fair to simply condemn the Chinese negotiators for their weakness or put blame on the diplomats of late Qing and on Robert Hart.

In fact, Hart heaved a sigh of relief. His goals had been reached. War was averted and the Chinese Customs, particularly his own position, was consolidated and strengthened.

Chapter Six

Hart's political crisis was over, but his family crisis had just begun.

While his marriage with Hester Bredon lasted 45 years until Hart's death, they lived together for only thirteen of those years. From the age of 41, Hart lived a celibate life in Beijing for more than thirty years.

He naturally wanted to have a normal family life, but his wife found life in an alien land hard to bear on a long-term basis. Her aversion to Beijing's harsh and dry winter, and its dust storms in spring, was quite understandable. In 1875, nine years into their marriage, Mrs. Hart decided to take the children and leave China the following spring.

She had every reason to want to go back to Britain. Their daughter was five years old and would soon be going to school, and doubtlessly their children should receive a British education. But there was another important reason for her decision to return to Britain, or rather a feeling that something else was going on, although she had no specific evidence.

The Harts' marriage was well into its ninth year, and it had been almost ten years since he sent Anna, Herbert and Arthur Hart—his children by Ayao—to Britain. It was Smith, Elder & Company that committed the children to the charge of its bookkeeper's wife, Mrs. Davidson. Anna was now sixteen, Herbert thirteen, and Arthur soon to be ten. It was time to make arrangements for their future.

Hart planned to send the two boys to board at the Junior School of Clifton College. They could later be trained for the Indian Civil Service. As for Anna, he wanted her to be sent to a Protestant boarding school on the European continent where she would be comfortably lodged and well treated, and could devote herself to three years' study of music, French and German. He asked Campbell to take care of this private matter for him. Since Campbell was the director of the Chinese Customs' London office and also his best friend, he was the safest person to do this. Hart enclosed a 300-pound check as initial payment for the arrangements.

Acting upon Hart's behest, Campbell located Mrs. Davidson to see how well Hart's three children were doing. He wrote back to Hart, telling him that Herbert was a strong healthy boy with ruddy cheeks, looking English except for his hair and eyes, that Anna with her freckles looked more Chinese, and Arthur thoroughly so and rather delicate. They treated Mrs. Davidson as their very own mother, and Mrs. Davidson said that she loved them just as she did her own. Campbell believed she did. The children looked happy, spoke nicely and had good manners. Anna played polka and mazurka on the piano for Campbell, "accurately but without showing much musical feeling."[19] But Mrs. Davidson was annoyed with the plans for the children's sudden removal. Having lived for nine years with Hart's children, she loved them, especially Anna. But there was nothing she could do. She was in no position to disrupt Hart's plans for his children.

But why did Hart do as he did? Was it for the sake of his children or for himself? Since he could not personally bring up the children, he should have been grateful to the family that took them in and especially the mistress of the house who loved them. He did admit that she was very nice to them. It was true that they had not *turned geniuses*, but from her letters, Hart judged Anna to be *rather well taught*.

Why didn't Hart want the children to stay with that family? With a mind that embraced even the smallest details, he must have had good reasons for that decision.

As Hart wished, Campbell took Herbert and Arthur to Clifton College, but they failed the entrance examination so Campbell had to enroll them in a private school run by the Reverend Bird. Anna got into a Miss Peile's school in Switzerland to study French and music.

Hart was bitterly disappointed with the boys but what could he do?

These arrangements were made behind his wife's back, of course, but Mrs. Hart seemed to have sensed something. Women's intuition in these matters is inscrutable. In his meticulousness Hart thought he had left no traces of what he did, and yet she may not have needed evidence in her suspicions. She could not put her finger on anything specific. She just said that she wanted to go back and there was no room for discussion.

Hart's feelings were mixed. Ayao would have stayed with him if she had been in Hessie's position. Of course, there was no "if." Everything was history now, only it was by no means easy to bury the past. The three children of Hart and Ayao were growing up day by day. They were his flesh and blood. In the stillness of the night, Hart would feel surges of guilt as he lay in bed, staring at the gray ceiling. He had not done a father's duty by them in so many years. Although compared with many shameless scoundrels, he was quite decent. He paid for their living and education expenses and sent them to good schools. But the children were denied what was most important to them: a relationship with their parents. Hart bore their expenses not as a father but as a guardian; he had never even written a letter to them so as not to leave a paper trail. For someone with his learning and good sense, he should have known that nothing hurts children more than separation from their parents.

Three years later, Hart went back to Europe and stayed for

one year. This was his first journey back to Britain since the time he took his three children by Ayao to Britain twelve years earlier. In that relatively leisurely period of time, he was troubled by conflicting feelings. Those three children were his flesh and blood after all, the products of love between him and the most "amiable and sensible woman". [20] But he was now with his new family, taking his wife and children on tours around Europe. He was wealthy enough to let them stay in the best hotels, enjoy the best food and beverages, and live in the lap of luxury. But he could not stifle his thoughts about the other three children or suppress his guilt. How he wished to visit them and see how they were doing. He only had Campbell's reports.

He wanted to see them for himself, but it would not do to humor those fancies. Someone of high status, a politician in a unique position like him in particular, had to sacrifice part of his private life. As the children had grown up, it was necessary to take extra precautions.

Hart took care of the children through Campbell who, in his turn, relied on the services of a lawyer named Hutchins. Hutchins had no inkling as to the true relationship between Hart and the children. Realizing that it was impossible to find another family willing to take them, he recommended that they be returned to Mrs. Davison who loved them. This was indeed a reasonable suggestion but, after brief moments of hesitation, Hart flatly rejected it. He wrote, "Anywhere rather than London, and any people rather than the Davidsons. If the boy is not fit for an office, let him go to sea or some such way of gaining his livelihood: I mean the youngest. Of course I want to do the best possible for these youngsters: but we cannot go beyond *possibilities*, and they must rough it. I fear they have been to too high-class schools hitherto. I do hope you'll manage some way of settling them. All that is necessary is to find something for them to do by which, with what they have got, they may live. ... If necessary apprentice them in shops: you can make a druggist of one, a woolen-draper of the other. ... I repeat, I am of opinion that away from London and not with the Davidsons might be best."[21]

The reason he repeatedly emphasized that they were not to live in London and not with the Davidsons was precisely that the children had been staying with the Davidsons since they arrived in England. Hart was in great fear that his relationship with the children would come to light. His good name being very important to him, he did not want to be the subject of gossip and wished with all his heart to avoid all contact with them.

Four years later, Hart instructed Campbell to send Herbert, who was quite a grown-up by then, to Canada or another British colony. In short, get the boy as far away from him as possible!

Chapter Seven

On July 14, 1883, two French warships sailed majestically into the Mawei naval port of Fujian. The port was adjacent to Mawei Shipyard, the largest shipyard in the Far East, established in 1866 by Zuo Zongtang and Shen Baozhen with the help of French officer Prosper Giguel after three years of preparation.

The Chinese at Mawei were not on guard against the French warships. It would never have occurred to them that the French, who had helped them build the shipyard, would now be there to destroy it. However China and France were, in fact, in a state of hostilities at this time. Armed clashes had already erupted on the border of China and Vietnam. Probably due to the backwardness of communication facilities, Mawei of Fuzhou, far removed from the battlefield, was a scene of peace and tranquility.

Hoisting colorful flags, the French warships slowly sailed into the port under the blazing July sun. The French crew members indicated through flag signals to their Chinese counterparts that the cheerful decorations were in honor of the Chinese Emperor's birthday. The Chinese were delighted, and indeed they were used to receiving tributes from foreigners on the occasion of imperial birthday celebrations. The fact France had never been a vassal state of China did not exclude the possibility there might be sensible French minds that understood the ways of the Chinese court. The Chinese always treated friends with proper decorum.

At eight o'clock in the morning on August 23, the consuls of all countries in Fuzhou received a notice from France declaring war against China. Two hours later, the notification was delivered to He Jing, Viceroy of Fujian and Zhejiang. With alacrity, the Viceroy relayed the news to Zhang Peilun, Commissioner of Coastal Defense, and He Ruzhang, Commissioner of Naval Affairs of Fujian.

It was a bolt out of the blue. How could friends who had come to offer congratulations declare war in the twinkling of an eye? He Ruzhang in his naivety said that the Chinese warships were not yet battle-ready and proposed asking the French to postpone the war by one day. He was still thinking as one did in antiquity. Sure enough, at noontime, the chief of the Fujian Naval Affairs Bureau sent a reply to the French, asking for postponement of the battle. As to be expected, the French refused. Only then did He Ruzhang hasten to have ammunition delivered to the Chinese warships.

The military strength was highly unbalanced. The French had eight warships, of which two were ironclads and two were torpedo vessels, with a total tonnage of 14,514. They had 1,790 officers and men and 77 heavy guns. The Chinese had eleven boats, of which nine were made of wood, with a total tonnage of only 6,500, and 45 guns, most of which were of small caliber. To make matters worse, the Chinese Viceroy happened to be such a fool. How in the world were they going to win the war?

At 1:56 that very afternoon, the French warship the *Lynx* opened fire first. The Chinese *Zhenwei* fired back. In less than one minute, the Chinese corvette *Yangwu* was hit by a torpedo and sank. Within one hour almost all the Chinese warships had been sunk. At 2:25 the docks of Mawei Shipyard were destroyed in the gunfire, and the very next day the entire shipyard, established by Zuo Zongtang with 30 million taels of silver and with help from France, was demolished.

China was forced to declare war on France.

The Inspector General's brass band had been long out of practice and the I. G. had not thrown a party in a long time. In no mood for festivity he had shut himself up in his room. His spacious mansion was cheerless and still.

Hart had learned about the Mawei hostilities the moment they started. The advanced communications system of the Customs Service kept him informed at all times. Even though the Zongli Yamen had not yet approached him, he knew they would. He needed to be prepared and come up with a proposal to cope with the situation.

He had just returned from Shanghai on a visit to the new French Minister Patenôtre to start diplomatic mediation efforts at the request of the Zongli Yamen. On July 19, the Qing government had, at Hart's request, sent Zeng Guoquan, Minister Plenipotentiary, to Shanghai for negotiations. After the Shanghai talks failed, the Zongli Yamen turned to the United States government for its assistance, but nothing had come of that either. On August 5, France dispatched a flotilla, commanded by Sébastien Lespès, to attack Jilong of Taiwan but met with strong resistance from the local troops led by Liu Mingchuan. It was then that the French turned their guns to Fujian. So the Mawei Incident did not come as a surprise to Hart.

French forces had entered Annam (present-day Vietnam) at the beginning of the nineteenth century. By 1880 France had deployed troops in Hanoi and Hai Phong, building fortresses along the Red River banks.

Annam had been a vassal state of China. In order to resist the French invasion, the government of Annam continued to pay tribute to China and asked for assistance from a group known as the Chinese Black Flag irregulars, stationed on the Annamese border. In 1882, the Black Flag Army began fighting the French, and in 1883, the Qing government's regular army entered Tonkin.

The Chinese government was in a dilemma if they wanted the Chinese troops to advance. Chinese military strength was all too clearly inferior to the French, and there was also the possibility of other Western powers making a move when Chinese forces were otherwise engaged. They were likely to go two steps back for every one forward. But withdrawal meant not only abandoning Annam's status as a vassal state of China but also exposing the provinces of Yunnan and Guangxi to French forces and, at the same time, triggering a chain reaction in Korea and Tibet.

Li Hongzhang and Prince Gong were in favor of a peaceful settlement. They did not think that the nascent Chinese navy was likely to emerge victorious, and felt that the only alternative was to bide time and react when under attack. Zeng Jize, the Chinese Minister to France, believed that France, with its volatile domestic political situation, was isolated on the European political stage and was therefore unable to sustain a war overseas. He pushed for a hard line. Some young Chinese officials calling themselves the "party of the Purists" [Qingliu] were even more hawkish, asserting that morally speaking, China must fight even if it knew it was going to lose. Each of these three schools of thought had its justifications, thus leading to indecision on the part of the highest policy makers.

In France the hawks prevailed. The hawkish Jules Ferry formed his cabinet for the second time on February 1, 1883. In his view, Frédéric Bourée, the French Minister to China, had failed in his negotiations with Li Hongzhang in December of 1882, so he recalled Bourée and named Aurthur Tricou, French Minister to Japan, as the new French envoy extraordinaire to China. In April, Ferry submitted to the French Parliament a military budget involving 5.5 million francs for an expeditionary force to Tonkin. With its adoption on May 15, 1883, France had eliminated all barriers to a war in the Far East.

On December 11, a 5,000-strong French contingent led by Admiral Amédée Courbet, the newly appointed commander of the expeditionary force, departed from Hanoi. And so the Sino-French War began. In February 1884, Millot replaced Courbet as commander-in-chief of the expeditionary force, troop strength was increased to 16,000, and all the important strongholds in Annam were taken by the French.

Hart was also in favor of a peaceful settlement. On November 7, 1883, at the last moment of the Sino-French diplomatic war, Hart stated this view in a letter to the Zongli Yamen, but he did not receive a reply. His superiors could not come to a decision, and he knew that the more indecisive they were, the more they needed him.

He became particularly concerned about the German, Detring. In March 1884, Detring was transferred to Guangzhou to be Commissioner of the Customs there. After arriving in Hong Kong, the Deputy Commander of the French Far East Fleet Lespès invited him to go to Guangzhou on the French cruiser, the *Volta*. This invitation was loaded with meaning. The *Volta*'s captain Francois-Ernest Fournier had been a longtime resident of Tianjin, where Detring had worked in the Customs for many years. They were old acquaintances and both knew Li Hongzhang.

Riding on the crest of its military victories, France took advantage of this personal connection and proposed to reopen negotiations but, as victor on the battlefield, set forth a precondition for the talks: The hard-line Chinese Minister to France, Zeng Jize, must be transferred elsewhere. Detring sent a telegram to Li informing him of this development. Li then asked the Zongli Yamen to order Hart to reappoint Detring to Tianjin for important business.

Wondering if this was an unauthorized decision by the French navy, Hart sent a telegram to Campbell, asking him to go secretly to Paris at once to find out about the real intentions of the French government. Hart didn't know that the Chinese government had already accepted the demand for the recall of

Zeng Jize.

On May 8, the French Prime Minister sent a coded telegram to naval captain Fournier, giving him full powers as a negotiator. Three days later, on May 11, Li and Fournier signed the *Articles of the Tientsin* (Tianjin) *Accord* after only two or three hours of talks. Such a speedy agreement was rare in diplomatic negotiations. The agreement meant that the Qing government would recognize all French treaties with Annam, and withdraw Chinese troops from Tonkin. The French promised not to demand an indemnity. The agreement also established free traffic in goods between Annam and France on the one part and China on the other, under a commercial and customs treaty to be drawn up "under the most advantageous conditions possible for French commerce."

Soon thereafter, in June, French lieutenant colonel Alphonse Dugenne led a 900-strong contingent on orders to take Langson, the strategic town on the Annamese border with Guangxi. On June 13, the French encountered Qing troops at Bodhisattva Bridge, Bac Le. The Qing commander Huang Yuxian notified Dugenne by letter that he had received no instructions to withdraw, and very reasonably asked him to send a heliograph message back to Hanoi to seek instructions. Without a competent interpreter able to grasp the subtleties of the Chinese message, Dugenne immediately mounted an attack but it failed. French casualties ran to nearly a hundred.

On June 30, the French chargé d'affaires Semalle met Yikuang, also known as Prince Qing, minister of the Zongli Yamen. Accusing him of violating the Articles of the Tianjin Accord, he demanded an indemnity of 250 million francs and threatened to launch naval attacks against Fujian and Taiwan.

Not knowing how to deal with this unexpected turn of events, the Qing government asked Hart to mediate. That very day, Hart went to the French Legation. Semalle told him that the French action was legitimate because Li and Fournier had agreed on the withdrawal of the Chinese troops on the Guangxi border by June 6 and the Chinese troops on the

Yunnan border by June 26. The following afternoon Hart went to the Zongli Yamen to see ministers Wu Tingfen and Zhang Yinhuan and relayed the words of the French chargé d'affaires. Wu and Zhang replied that the Chinese troops had not withdrawn sooner because the Articles did not specify the dates of withdrawal nor did Li's letters.

This had become a baffling case.

On July 12, the French chargé d'affaires issued an ultimatum to the Zongli Yamen, demanding a reply within seven days, and the next day, Rear Admiral Alexandre Louis Francais Peyron, French Minister of the Navy and the Colonies, said in a telegram to Courbet, "Dispatch all the vessels at your disposal to Fuzhou and Jilong. Our plan is to take these two ports as hostages, if our ultimatum is rejected."

On September 11, Hart sent a telegram through Campbell to Rendel, member of the British Parliament, seeking advice on whether or not it was possible for Britain to join Germany in appealing to both China and France to accept the United States' mediation. A week later, on September 18, Hart sent another telegram to Campbell, asking him to undertake a clandestine trip to Paris to see Jules Ferry, Prime Minister of France. The very next day, he telegraphed to say there was no need for a Paris trip, but Campbell had already gone, though he did not get to see the Prime Minister.

Hart, after all, was an official serving the Chinese imperial court. He would not have frivolously acted on his own initiative in sending his representative to see the head of government of the country at war with China. He was not a reckless man. He was acting on the orders of the Chinese government, to test the waters in his unique capacity. However the divergence of views at the highest echelons of the Qing court made things difficult for him.

The Sino-French War was still going on. The French Navy had turned their spearhead toward Taiwan but their military offensive did not go smoothly. France and Britain had clashes of interest on Egypt in the first place, and military operation along China's coastline could not very well go ahead in total disregard of the other powers' attitudes. France did not have absolute predominance in this war.

At the beginning of October, when the Chinese government was resentful toward the United States and Germany for advising China to pay the indemnity, Hart thought that Britain could try a different tack and advise China to reject the idea. This would provide a good opportunity to establish a long-lasting alliance with China. A Sino-British alliance was what Hart most wanted to see, but he was in no position to call the shots in the British government. On October 25, Hart telegraphed Campbell, asking him to sound out Granville, the British Foreign Secretary, through Rendel, member of the House of Commons, and ascertain the real intentions of the British government. Campbell's reply came after three days. The British government wished for a cessation of the Sino-French hostilities.

The Empress Dowager's sudden summons picked up Hart's spirits. He knew her importance in China, and also knew she would not step to the front unless it was absolutely necessary.

The Empress Dowager Cixi had just moved from Lasting Spring Hall to the newly renovated Hall of Beauties. It was October, and there had recently been a lavish ceremony in celebration of her fiftieth birthday. The other two nearby halls in the same compound, with their newly installed hardwood carved partition screens and nanmu wood carved doors and windows, also shone in their elegant splendor.

Walking down the alley leading to the living quarters of the palace, Hart could sense the approach of a historic opportunity.

At such a critical juncture, no one but the power-monopolizing Empress Dowager Cixi could brush aside Li Hongzhang, the veteran diplomat, and Zeng Jize, the Chinese Minister to France, and entrust the destiny of the country to a foreigner.

In the last few months of 1884, China and France were at loggerheads on both military and diplomatic fronts. On China's part, there were regrettable actions that had exacerbated the situation. For example, some officials in Guangzhou put up posters encouraging the sale of poisoned grain and rice to French merchants. Such actions made Hart worry that international public opinion might turn toward the French. But generally speaking, China was holding up well and did not turn out to be as weak as the West had imagined. Even Hart said that although he was in favor of a peaceful settlement, his sympathies were entirely with the hawkish ministers. If he were Chinese, he would *fight it out*.[22]

In those days, Hart *had not had a minute for ordinary Customs business. With the "house on fire," it is hard to go on "baking bread" as usual*.[23] He was trying to persuade the Chinese government to accept British assistance, and on November 11, China did officially indicate willingness to accept British mediation. From November 16 to November 18, Hart sent six telegrams to Campbell, repeatedly stating China's terms. Hart hoped with all his heart for the success of the British mediation. From his point of view, this would serve to avoid any losses that a war might inflict on the Chinese Customs and, at the same time, to improve relations between the two countries. That would be a win-win result for him.

But the month-long British mediation failed to lead to substantial results.

China soon had new worries, as on December 4, the Insurrection of 1884 broke out in Korea, a failed three-day coup d'état that led to clashes between the Chinese and Japanese armies. Worries about being exposed to attacks from far and near softened the Chinese position in the negotiations.

On December 14, the Zongli Yamen accepted Hart's proposal to add to the Li-Fournier Convention a reasonably argued interpretative article, but also pointed out that this position was not to be publicized so as not to appear too eager to seek peace. Hart agreed. In diplomatic negotiations, it was unwise to let the other side find out about your bottom line. The negotiations must be very subtle. These were conducted through the British Foreign Office, with Hart playing a front-line position.

It was snowing outside. Unable to see anything through the window, Hart wanted to take a walk in the courtyard. As he opened the door, the icy wind almost choked him but still he stepped out, leaving deep footprints in the snow. It was New Year's Eve, a joyous time in Britain, but Hart was in no mood for festivities. Even if there had been a New Year party, he would not have gone. He hoped the chill of the wind and the snow would inspire him to find a way to talk directly with the top leaders of France. But there was little chance of that. How could a British subject in the role of I. G. of the Chinese Customs serve as the highest representative of the Chinese government?

He went back to his room. On his desk stood piles of Customs documents claiming his attention. With the Sino-French war still going on, Customs matters, however urgent, had been pushed to the backburner. As he absent-mindedly leafed through the pages, suddenly one report caught his eye. Two months earlier, the French navy had detained a Chinese Customs' revenue cruiser *Flying Tiger* [Feihoo] delivering supplies to lighthouses. The French commander Courbet notified the Chinese Customs that he was not going to release the boat unless Hart went in person to Paris and obtained authorization there.

Such an excessive demand could very well have been taken as something quite normal considering the two countries were at war. Hart's subordinate who had reported the matter did not think that Hart would travel all the way to Paris for the sake of a supplies boat. But it suddenly occurred to Hart that the French commander might have had other things in mind in demanding his presence in Paris.

"Could this have been a diplomatic initiative by the

highest French authorities? Even if the French were not thinking along those lines, could the opportunity be seized and turned to our favor?" Hart wondered. He realized that this was the moment for him to take center stage. In his excitement, he lost no time in sending a telegram to Campbell, instructing him to immediately go on a secret visit to Paris as his private representative and ask to see Prime Minister Ferry, to discuss the matter of the *Flying Tiger*.

When Ferry and Campbell met on January 11, 1885 in Palais Bourbon, their conversation focused solely on the Chinese Customs' boat *Flying Tiger*. Not a word was said on the Sino-French peace talks. Clearly a little revenue cruiser was not worthy of a prime minister's time. But using indirect means to get around to the main purpose is a standard diplomatic strategy, and establishment of direct contact with the highest authorities of France was a major breakthrough. Hart was satisfied.

On a mid-January Sunday, Hart took a high-spirited long walk in his garden in Beijing, the first time in three months that he did so in bright sunlight. As he strolled along, he recited poetry aloud, his heart flooded with joy. Things were going well.

Campbell met with Ferry four times on January 25, February 6, February 20, and February 24 and their talks eventually turned to France's relations with China. Campbell relayed Hart's messages and laid out terms acceptable to the Chinese government. While the negotiations were going on, the French troops intensified their attacks in Annam, capturing Langson on February 14 and Wenyuanzhou on February 23. The Qing government was compelled to yield more ground in the negotiations.

The Chinese Emperor now ordered that authorities in Tianjin, Shanghai, Fuzhou and Guangzhou halt negotiations in their tracks so as not to hamper Hart's efforts. *Amateur diplomacy*[24] had now acquired official status and had become the only game in town. By March, the negotiations had basically concluded. On March 22, Li Hongzhang issued a note through diplomatic channels authorizing Hart and his representative Campbell to make all decisions. While a Chinese military victory at Langson on March 8 led to Jules Ferry's downfall, the changes in the French political establishment did not alter the results of the negotiations. On April 4, the Sino-French Ceasefire Agreement was signed by James Campbell on behalf of the Chinese government and Albert Billot, director of political affairs of the French Foreign Office.

The main reasons for the peace agreement were practicalities on each side. The rice embargo and the conclusion of the French Treaty with Burma in January 1885 had increased tension in Anglo-French relations, and the protracted war of aggression in Madagascar had bred widespread discontent among the French populace. Therefore France urgently needed to extricate itself from the quagmire of war in China. And on China's part, the government had incurred foreign debt seven times in order to meet military expenses as well as having to deal with Japan after the Korean coup d'état. So China was also eager for peace. Nevertheless, the role played by Hart and Campbell in the negotiations must not be overlooked, and Hart was elated by the success.

Hart was standing in front of his tall desk which had a slanted writing board as he made a habit of writing while standing at his desk. His servant entered with a calling card. The visitor was Brinkley, captain of the Royal Artillery, who had long settled in Japan, and was now visiting China as the chief advisor to the Japanese Minister Plenipotentiary Ito Hirobumi. He had arrived in Beijing only the night before.

Hart did not go immediately to the reception room. Before he saw his visitor, he needed time to think. Ito, an important figure in Japanese reforms in modern history, was at that time already a leading statesman. Six months later, after Japan adopted the cabinet system, he was to become its first Prime Minister. He was now in China to talk about the Sino-Japanese conflict subsequent to the Korean coup d'état of December 1884. The success or failure of the talks would be of crucial importance to China as well. What was of particular concern to Hart was a private conversation between Ito and the French Minister Patenôtre when Ito was passing by Shanghai. What had they talked about? Would Japan act in collusion with France? Would his arrival undermine the Sino-French peace talks on the eve of their success?

Hart and Brinkley chatted amicably in the reception room well lit by the cozy winter sun. The two British subjects, one representing Japan, the other representing China, were trying to sound each other out in their pleasant conversation. This is the stuff drama is made of.

Hart was of course much more experienced than Brinkley, but he was troubled by the thought that the British Minister to China, Harry Parkes, with his *Japanese proclivities, would make difficulties for China* in the Sino-Japanese negotiations.[25] At such moments, Hart's feelings toward his own country defied description.

At this point, the servant entered again, carrying a silver tray with a letter in it. Only communications requiring immediate attention could be brought in while the master was with visitors. Hart knew it must be urgent, and opened it with a letter-opener. It was a very simple note from Nicholas Frederick O'Conor, chief counselor of the British Legation, informing him that Parkes had died of malaria a few hours earlier in Beijing.

Hart cast a glance at the clock on the wall and saw that it was 10:10 am; the date was March 22, 1885. Without betraying his emotions, he put the note back into the envelope and marveled at the vicissitudes and the coincidences of life. He said to himself that maybe this was God's work.

Hart would never have imagined that, a week later, on March 30, the British government would decide to have him succeed Parkes as the British Minister.

Hart heard about this at Parkes' funeral. This should

have been wonderful news to him. Granted that the I. G. of the Chinese Imperial Maritime Customs was already quite an impressive rank, he was after all an official of a foreign country, a weak country that the haughty English looked down on. Thirty years had elapsed since he was recruited by the British Foreign Office in 1854 at the age of nineteen. A post as a special minister plenipotentiary would have been the peak of his expectations as a young man joining the consular service, and it was evidence of the British government's full recognition of his abilities. Moreover, he had always been dissatisfied with British diplomats who, with their slowness and inefficiency, had let go of many opportunities that could have been advantageous to Britain.

He should not have had any second thoughts. But he had been working in the Customs for upwards of twenty years and, being the de facto founder of the new Chinese Customs, he felt an inseparable bond with it.

After turning the matter over and over in his mind for more than twenty days, Hart sent a *strictly and wholly confidential* telegram to his wife on April 21: "British Government has offered me position of Minister Plenipotentiary here: Tsung-li Yamen urge acceptance: compliance entails prolonged stay in China, less pay, and probably without pension, but gives opportunity for perhaps useful work and wind up China career nicely. Would the honour etc. compensate for loss etc. What do you wish me to do? accept or decline? You can consult Rendel, but reply please to-morrow. I must telegraph my final decision immediately."[26]

Mrs. Hart's reply on April 23 was: "Accept appointment and telegraph to London immediately."

The telegram from his wife did not help him make up his mind, partly because he was being snowed under with work. After Campbell and Billot signed the ceasefire agreement, Li Hongzhang and Patenôtre, French Minister to China, were to start negotiating a formal treaty. But Hart and Campbell were afraid that Patenôtre would throw obstacles in the way and make the talks fall through at the last minute. So Hart proposed that Campbell continue the negotiations in Paris with G. Cogordan, who had replaced Billot in the new French cabinet.

The details were actually much more complicated. The officials in France would give the draft articles to Campbell, who would send them to Hart by telegraph. Hart would then submit them to the Zongli Yamen for the highest authorities to propose amendments, about which Hart would instruct Campbell to talk with Cogordan. After both parties reached agreement on some articles, the document would go to Li Hongzhang and Patenôtre for them to complete the details and check the wording. Hart was grateful that the Chinese government placed such trust in him even after he had been named as the next British Minister. This might have been one of the reasons for his hesitation in accepting the post.

Li Hongzhang and Patenôtre, understandably displeased at being reduced to an editing role, created some minor problems, but there was little they could do because the Empress Dowager was behind Hart. She reviewed each proposal of his in advance and was a strong advocate for peace. On June 9, 1885, Li Hongzhang and Patenôtre signed in Tianjin the Sino-French Treaty on Annam on behalf of their respective governments.

On June 23, the British government handed Hart the letter appointing him as the British Minister to China as well as his credentials to be presented to the Chinese Emperor, thus effectively sealing the deal. The next course of action was to pick his successor as the I. G.

Hart's proposed successor was his younger brother James Hart, but in fact James was by no means the right candidate. Even if he were not a playboy, which he was, it would be awkward to have brothers occupying two such important posts. The Chinese high-level officials would feel insecure, and relationships with other countries would also be difficult.

Li Hongzhang did not mince words in his objections.

He recommended the German, Detring, Commissioner of Customs. The other candidate was the American William Alexander Parsons Martin, president of the Tongwen Guan, the College of Interpreters.

Even though Martin was an old friend, Hart still felt it would be better for him to give up the post of minister if it meant that the post of I. G. were to fall into foreign hands. Moreover, he continued to argue, although the Zongli Yamen would be happy to see him as the next British Minister, the Empress Dowager wanted him to stay on as the I.G.. He decided to ask if he could gratefully turn down the offer of the post of British Minister and stay on as the I. G. in case he was not able to find a satisfactory successor.

The reply from the British Foreign Office came later that very day, telling him that his younger brother had been confirmed as his successor as the I. G. This meant that the British government must have communicated with the Chinese government in advance. By mid August, when Hart knew for sure that his brother would assume the I.G. role, he issued a Customs circular on August 15, announcing his departure and expressing his regret at the severance of his ties with the Customs. On the same day, he wrote a letter to his American friend Edward Bangs Drew, saying that in his preparations for his departure, he was experiencing the bitter taste of his success, as if he were dying before his time was up.

Hart picked an auspicious day, August 22, to take up his post in the British Legation. It was his wedding anniversary, and he had been I. G. for exactly 22 years.

But James Hart had not shown up. Robert Hart had to hand over the Customs work to James before he could officially assume his new post. Recalling his life as the I. G. over the last twenty years, he was overwhelmed by a surge of mixed feelings. Plus, to hand over such massive duties to a newcomer was a daunting task. A sudden thought occurred to him: Was James able to take over such heavy responsibilities and such a grueling work schedule? He could have hired assistants but he never did. He gave personal attention to everything because he didn't trust anyone. Could he trust James? Of course there was no need to doubt his brother's loyalty to him but this was not a question of loyalty. James would never work the way he did. James was a fun-loving person, likely to ruin the Customs kingdom that he had painstakingly built from scratch!

Hart was in no mood to sort out the important documents that must be handed over. He picked up his violin and hit a false note, shaking his head. His servant then came in and announced a visitor.

To his surprise, it was his old friend Mr. Martin! He had long been wishing to talk things over with Martin, and yet, with Martin being one of the candidates to succeed him, it had not been possible to do so. At this point, his mind flashed back to the time long ago when they were talking on top of the city wall of Ningbo. Martin was after all a trustworthy friend, a friend he could talk to.

Martin was clearly not here for a casual chat. He took a sip of coffee and waited for the servant to leave the reception room before he said, "So you've made up your mind?"

Hart looked at him without saying anything.

Martin continued, "I'm neither an Englishman nor a Chinese. For me to comment on this matter with you is to poke my nose into something that doesn't concern me."

"Oh, but I'm all ears!"

Martin laughed. "You're not being truthful! Aren't you already about to report to work at the Legation? Don't tell me you are all ears!"

With a sigh, Hart said, "Yes, I *am* about to take up my post, but I still don't feel comfortable with the idea."

"I know," said Martin, nodding. "Otherwise I wouldn't have come. I understand. To be a British Minister is an honor one can hardly refuse."

"But you are here to talk me into turning it down."

"How do you know?"

"Then what exactly brought you here?"

Both burst out laughing.

"Tell me, why shouldn't I be a British Minister?"

"If you leave your current post, pandemonium will break out in the Customs."

"Aren't you overstating it?"

"No. I mean it. Is your choice, James, the right candidate?"

Hart fell silent.

"I say this to you because we are old friends. No other person would dare to, least of all your subordinates. But they will be resentful. I say he is not the right candidate. This isn't because he is your brother. If someone is capable, it doesn't matter if there's resentment. Power coupled with wisdom would be enough to win people over, just as you did when you first took up this post in your twenties. There was a lot of resentment at the time, but you brought people around. But it won't be the same with James."

Hart slowly stirred his coffee with his spoon.

"You don't think I'm right?"

"You are right. To tell you the truth, the first one to be resentful may be my best friend in the Customs."

"Campbell?"

"Yes, Campbell. He made a good showing as a skillful diplomat in the French negotiations. There's no lack of people in the public who believe he'll be my successor, but I never mentioned his name when he and I talked about the succession. But he's not the right candidate, either. What's more, he can't leave London. He has his family to take care of, and he knows that. But, yes, he will be resentful if James takes over."

With a nod, Martin said, "The post of I. G. is too much of a challenge, much more so than the post of British Minister! Anybody can be a minister, but you are the only one who can do the job of an I. G."

"Surely it's not as bad as that! I know that some people recommended you."

"I mean what I said. I'm not up to this job, and I'm not being modest. An I. G. must balance not just the interests of

China and Britain, but also the economic interests of other countries in their dealings with China as well as with Britain. And then there are the intricate relationships with Chinese officialdom, the relations between the Zongli Yamen and the Empress Dowager. ... It's mind-boggling! I can't imagine how you've been doing all this so well all these years!"

With a deep sigh, Hart said, "You are the only one who understands me! No one has ever said this to me!"

Martin continued, "Just think, should the Customs be thrown into chaos, you as the British Minister will also have a tough time—you who know the Customs well and whose brother is the I. G.! How are you going to iron out all the complications? There'll be nothing you can do about the Customs as a minister representing British interests only. And you will do poorly as a representative of British interests, thus failing on both fronts—in fact, on multiple fronts!"

Hart's eyes lit up in sudden enlightenment. "This is truly a case of 'The spectator sees the game best!'"

Martin laughed. "A smart man like you shouldn't need me to give you pointers. The famous Song Dynasty poet Su Dongpo put it well: 'I fail to see the true face of Mount Lushan, because I myself am in the mountain.'"

"Yes, that's Chinese wisdom. All right, I'll do as you say! No minister for me! Now let me treat you to a drink. This is the best whisky there is!"

At the end of August, Hart announced his decision to stay at the Customs.

Chapter Eight

Whether one chalks it up to a sense of responsibility or an obsession with fame and glory, by 1891, Hart had been working for 37 years in China. And a good part of the time he was alone. Hessie and the two children had not returned to China since their departure ten years earlier.

With his intelligence and profound insight, Hart had trouble finding people to talk to. This only added to his loneliness. Little wonder why he kept writing long letters to Campbell.

A letter of February 26, 1891 particularly makes the reader's heart go out to him. "I have been having—not a fit of our English 'blues' exactly—but a spell of loneliness which is not quite the thing: there's plenty of society here and I am asked out often enough, but it's the same people and the same way of killing time everywhere and I'm so tired of it I stay at home, refuse to go out, read all the evening and, though intensely bored if anybody interrupts my regular reading or takes me out of my habits, begin to find that occupation is not everything and that family life would be far otherwise. To be alone as I am certainly helps me to see into oneself and to weigh many outside matters accurately and wisely: but it is a sort of solitary confinement with hard labour self-imposed. I have been too long at work, too long in China, too long alone—and I'm 'losing touch' with people too much."

He needed the emotional attachment of family, which was why when he learned two months later that Evey, his older daughter by Hessie, was coming to China, the news acted on him as sweet rain on parched earth. His dried-up soul felt rejuvenated. His longing for family life, all but extinguished, raised its head again. In all eagerness he wanted to know if his wife was also coming. He assumed she wouldn't but he still hoped for a miracle. He asked Campbell to sound Mrs. Hart out. But even if his daughter was coming alone, he was excited enough. The sudden advent of good news threw him into a flutter. He said, "As I last saw my children little people under ten and have since been living alone, I fear my paternal character will be at fault—separated from them, I have not matured in the same ratio!"[27]

He tried to visualize the scene of reunion, wrapped in the happiness that he was about to enjoy, but he did not lose his good judgment. He braced himself for the possibility that his wife would not show up. Sure enough, his wife had never even intended to come. There must be no interruption in the schooling of their son Bruce, who had the Chinese name He Chengxian, and their younger daughter Nollie, and she could not leave them to their own devices. These were highly convincing reasons but Hart was no less disappointed.

Be that as it may, his older daughter's coming breathed new life into Hart's humdrum routine. He began to imagine when Evey was to board her ship, who would be seeing her off at the wharf, and where her ship would be sailing past. He said, "What a change it will make in my life, my ten year's independence don't fit me for doing paterfamilias a bit I fear!"[28]

It came as a total surprise to him that Evey announced as soon as she arrived in Beijing that she was getting married. He froze as if doused with a bucketful of cold water. Joy had so turned his head that he had never even paused to ask himself why she was coming to China—exclusively to see him?

Her visit had of course been planned well in advance. She could not have fallen in love upon first sight of her groom-to-be in a casual meeting right after her arrival in Beijing. To add insult to injury, the groom-to-be was William Beauclerk, chief counselor in the British embassy in China, whom Hart knew. Beauclerk was a good twenty years older than Evey and was a widower with three children. Knowing he was not worthy of Evey, Beauclerk had kept this a water-tight secret from Hart until it was already a fait-accompli or, as the Chinese idiom goes, "The rice is already cooked."

What grieved Hart was the fact that even his daughter had not breathed a word of it to him. And he had been deluded into believing that she was here to see him! Wasn't he acting like an unrequited lover? But he was in no position to be angry with her. She was indeed of marriageable age. Had he ever cared about her marriage prospects? Had he ever done anything to find her a match? Living so far away, he had not done his fatherly duties by her. Now that she had made her choice and was in China for the wedding, he couldn't very well call things off. However angry and regretful he was, his rational mind told him to support the marriage. At least Beauclerk was from an eminent family and enjoyed good social status, or so rationalized Hart to himself resignedly.

He began placing large orders of clothes from London, pulling himself together with forced smiles in his preparations for the wedding. The girl whom he had been looking forward to seeing had thrown herself into the arms of another man. This was truly a hard pill for Hart to swallow. Any father would have mixed feelings at his daughter's wedding, let alone Hart with his hunger for affection.

The wedding was scheduled for September 5, so there wasn't much time. Afraid that what he had ordered for the wedding might not arrive in time, he ordered wedding cakes and clothes from Shanghai and Tianjin as well, as backups. To his relief, the shipment from England arrived one day in advance of the wedding. On September 4, the weather in

Beijing turned sunny and crisp, the best weather that Hart felt he had ever experienced in that city, and the good weather lasted for more than two weeks, until the newlyweds had finished their honeymoon in the suburban hills. This made Hart feel better. It looked like this marriage did have divine blessing, after all.

The famous vacation spot of Brighton is only 70 kilometers from London, and Mrs. Hart often took her children there. It was probably there in the early summer of 1892 that Bruce came to know Miss Caroline Moore Gillson. They spent a memorable summer in this beautiful little town by the sea. He had just been accepted by Oxford University. The two joyful events so turned the eighteen-year-old's head that he was at a loss as to what to do. The sun of early summer gilded the cream-colored houses along the seaside promenade, and the moist sea breezes from the English Channel stroked the young man's hot cheeks. Queens Street, the Castle Square, the Palace Pier, the Old Ship Hotel—all these famous attractions of Brighton would remember the golden laughs of the young lovers. We can safely say that Bruce at this time was in no mood for a quiet life on the campus of Oxford.

Hart seemed to have had a premonition. He had given his son the Chinese name of Chengxian, meaning "to succeed one's ancestors," but he regretted that his son did not appear to be as hardworking as he wished him to be. His son had acquired flaws typical of young men from rich families.

Hart was worried. On August 28, 1892, he wrote to Campbell, "I wish you'd look up Bruce. He has not been writing to me this last year and I fear he has gone in for some dissipation at Oxford and is paying the cost of it for I believe he is ill and owes it to the life led there. At his age he would probably conceal any sickness, and when 'wine, women and cigars' are concerned, a man makes a mistake who shuns his doctor! My long stay in China has cut me and my family *completely* asunder—I'm sorry to say; and I don't know who is to be asked to keep an eye on Bruce except yourself. Savez?"

However, soon after this letter was put in the mail, Campbell's own son died, and Hart did not want to bother his friend at this unfortunate time. So he himself wrote a letter, advising his son that the less he had "to do with wine, women and cigars—although all very delicious—at his age, the better."[29]

But Hart was too far away to be of any help. By December, he saw nothing for it but to beg Campbell again to help keep Bruce in line.

Hart's worries were not unjustified. Miss Gillson, whom the now nineteen-year-old Bruce was in love with, was three years older than he was, and he had failed the exams of the first term at the university. Campbell learned that Bruce was prepared to elope with the young woman should his mother try to block the marriage.

Drawing on his own youthful experience, Hart had concluded that romance and career didn't have to be mutually exclusive. He telegraphed his son and *encouraged him to try again*.[30]

But it was evident that Mrs. Hart was understandably not as calm as her husband. This marked the beginning of tragedy. If Hart had been in England with Bruce, there was a chance that the father-son relationship could still be remedied, but he was at the other end of the world and was not able to do more than telegraph a few words at a time. Such brief statements of principle don't go far in the management of domestic affairs. Relations between mother and son had soured to such a degree that they refused to see and to speak to each other. Bruce asked his uncle to tell his mother that he wanted to go to China immediately to see his father.

Mrs. Hart was understandably upset. She complained to Campbell about her son's lack of trust in her and told him that she was upset because Bruce had again been to Brighton where Miss Gillson was, without asking for her permission. Trying to console her, Campbell replied that a boy could confide many things in his father but not necessarily in his mother.

On Bruce's troubled romance, Hart began to demonstrate a leniency that was quite exceptional in a parent. His March 5 letter to Campbell said, "The pair may be admirably suited and our 'experience' may only ruin a good thing if we interfere! I shall write to him later on—so as not to disturb his studies before the June examination, and we'll then have it out. My position is simply this: marry if you like my dear boy—I question the wisdom of it, but it's your affair: only, before you go in for domestic happiness, think of the 'ways and means,' for, you know, you must yourself, support your wife and family! ... We have all to make our own lives and bear our own burthens[31] and there's a point at which parental solicitude must give way to children's rights. I neither worship, nor bind myself by society views: *humanity*'s bigger than 'society,' and the individual need not always be part of the machine."

These were words of wisdom. His argument remains quite valid even today, more than a hundred years later. He was a wise man. If he had not been the I. G. of Customs, he might even have become a great intellectual.

If not for the unpleasantness regarding Bruce's marriage, the year 1893 would have been a very auspicious year for Hart. The protracted Tibet negotiations finally came to a conclusion. The postal service that Hart had been looking forward to for many years had been set in motion. And what excited him most was the conferral of baronetcy from the British government. Henceforth the Hart family ranked themselves among the aristocracy. He was understandably thrilled that his childhood dream had become true.

But the sudden advent of the title changed Hart's attitude about his son's marriage. It occurred to him that the problem might not be as simple as he had imagined it to be. He reasoned, "If Bruce is run after in a calculating spirit, the G. family will be more inclined to hold on to him than to let him off after the List [the Queen's Birthday Honors List] is out! If

Bruce were thirty or self-supporting I should not oppose his wishes—or if the girl were only ten instead of twenty-two, but, as things are, it is my duty to interfere and to 'head him off' out of what may be detrimental."[32]

Hart's interference was lawful. English law permitted the warding of any minor resident in England upon application to the Court of Chancery. One purpose in such action was the prevention of a marriage opposed by the ward's parents. The court could refuse permission for a marriage that it deemed unsuitable.[33]

This legal approach was worked out by Hart and his London lawyer Hutchins. A forceful intervention was quite a far cry from his attitude in March. Apart from his new baronetcy, he had been turning his mind back and forth in the last two months over his own youth and passion for his first love Ayao. His attitude back in March had everything to do with his own life experience, as did his change of mind now. Hart's position as a realist, which had earned him such a firm foothold in Chinese officialdom, now gained the upper hand in his thoughts toward his son's marriage.

Hart and Campbell were skilled diplomats who had often collaborated to negotiate as representatives of a large country to solve thorny international disputes. For them, there was nothing easier than working together to deal with a minor, Bruce, and his supposed future father-in-law, Mr. Gillson, a mere dentist.

Acting upon Hart's behest, Hutchins and Campbell completed all the necessary legal procedures in only two days. The Court of Chancery ruled against all direct and indirect contact between Bruce and Miss Gillson.

It was cruel. Campbell was afraid that the blow would make Bruce fall apart. But Hart in his self-confidence thought that it had all blown over. His mind turned to his baronetcy and the tracing of his family roots. He painstakingly designed a family coat of arms in anticipation of the upcoming grand ceremony to celebrate his baronetcy.

Little did he know that his son and Mr. Gillson were preparing for a lawsuit against him, even though a court victory over the elder Hart would be quite a challenge. What was important was not victory or defeat but the very fact that a son was suing his father. After the court started to hear the case, Gillson's lawyer argued that Bruce's chances of graduation were being ruined because, rather than taking the graduation exam, he was going to China to see his father. As it turned out, Bruce did take and pass the first round of exams for his Oxford BA degree and with his father's permission, departed on July 12 for Beijing via the United States.

With everything going his way, Hart was in a good mood. Unaware of the gravity of Bruce's situation, he was lost in the happiness of gaining an aristocratic title. The frown that had been settled on his brow for many years had vanished.

Bruce arrived in Beijing on September 6. He had been a twelve-year-old boy upon leaving China seven years earlier, and most of his childhood had been spent in Beijing. Reliving memories of the blue autumn sky, the long pigeon whistles, the dark green pines and cypresses, the vermillion palace walls, the glazed tiles glittering under the sun, the bluish-gray brick walls of the quiet alleys and the alluring hawks of the peddlers, he calmed down under the soothing effect. The decision to come to Beijing was well-advised. Since there was no way he could resist his parents' strong will, which was backed by the law, Beijing was the best place to take shelter from his longing for Brighton.

Hart was overjoyed to see his son. He still had vivid memories of how he had taken Bruce riding as a child. September being the best season in Beijing, they could ride every day again. Was there anything more pleasant than giving free rein to their horses along straight aspen-lined roads toward the verdant West Hills in the setting sun?

They avoided any topic that might cause discomfort. The reunion after a seven-year separation was joyful. Hart rarely had opportunities to enjoy domestic bliss. He cherished the occasion and persuaded himself that he was in no rush, that he could afford to wait. And his son should be the one eager to try and talk him around.

One day went by, then another, and another. To Hart's surprise, his son also appeared to be in no hurry. Bruce occupied himself with touring the city and recapturing his childhood. At the dinner table, he talked with his father with gusto about the gold fish jars for sale at Liulichang Antiques Market and the falcons at Dashanlan, the Entrance Arch of the Front Gate Street and the flag shows at the Herbal King Temple fairs. With the enthusiasm of a teenager, he bought crickets and grasshoppers, and delicious local treats such as fermented mungbean milk, hawthorn fruits on sticks, chestnut cakes and jam-filled pastries.

Hart listened with keen interest all the while doubting his son could have forgotten all about Miss Gillson, the lawsuit and everything that had happened in London and Brighton. In fact, the more he avoided the subjects, the more evident it was that he had not forgotten them. His resentment was precisely the reason for this purposeful avoidance. With the young man so calm and betraying no emotion, Hart couldn't help but see him in a new light. He had thought that as long as Bruce came to China and sat face to face with him, he could surely talk the young man around. It now looked like he had underestimated his son.

Eventually, the father brought up the subject first.

"Have you broken with Miss Gillson?"

"For now, yes."

"For now? What about later?"

"I'll see about that after I reach adulthood."

"You'll look her up then?"

"That will be my business."

"My son, there are lots of good girls out there."

"How do you know she's not a good girl?"

"I didn't say that. It's just that ..."

"Father, let's talk about this after I've reached adulthood. Isn't my age the reason for your objections? I'd be better off having fun with kites and grasshoppers now."

Hart had never expected his son to have so much hidden strength. Instead of arguing with his father, he stayed quietly with him, *riding, fiddling, reading, and doing some Chinese.* Hart realized, "He's very nice with me—but his heart is set on marrying Miss G.!"[34] Bruce knew that in the end there was nothing his father could do. Hart knew this too: "He holds the 'big suit' and highest 'trump' and all I do is try and not let him establish his 'suit' or play that big 'trump'!"[35]

The blow his son dealt him was crushing. With the advent of the harsh Beijing winter, Hart again sank into low spirits and poor health.

He had been under treatment for a cold, loss of appetite and fever, and was *pretty well run down.* For a time he thought of *moving off in mid-March* but worried that his departure would affect postal work.[36]

As for Bruce, he was only putting a good face on his agony. The prolonged separation from his beloved Miss Gillson was more than he could bear. Rumors from England that the girl was likely to transfer her attentions elsewhere were the last straw. He told his father that he wanted to rush back to England and marry before the year was out.

Bruce, to whom the days dragged by like years, succumbed to illness. His mind filled with thoughts of his love across the ocean, he suffered from insomnia, headaches, dizzy spells and nausea. He ate little and stopped riding, playing the violin, reading and going out. He stayed indoors, confined to his bed.

Hart grew afraid. He was a rational man. Knowing that there was nothing he could do, he resignedly gave in.

In 1894, when Hart was plagued with worries about his son's marriage prospects, China—the country where he had chosen to make his life—was in the grip of another major crisis.

That spring, a peasant rebellion broke out in Gobu in Korea's Cholla Province, and by May 31, the rebels occupied the seat of Cholla Province. In consternation, the Korean king asked for military help from Yuan Shikai, Chinese Imperial Resident-general of Seoul, to suppress the uprising. The Japanese embassy in Korea sent an envoy to Yuan Shikai to offer support for sending Chinese troops to aid the Korean government. This was in fact a Japanese plot. No sooner had the Chinese entered Korea than Japan also dispatched forces into Korea to challenge them. On July 25, Japan launched an undeclared war against China, conducting sneak attacks against the Chinese navy and army. On August 1, Emperor Guangxu issued an edict declaring war against Japan, and on the same day, the Japanese Emperor also declared war. And so the *Jiawu* War broke out.[37]

Hart knew that the war had been deliberately provoked by Japan, and that justice was on the side of China. While he was totally supportive of China, he also saw all too clearly that the corrupt Qing government was no match for post-Meiji Reform Japan.

As Hart rode to the Zongli Yamen, the joltings of the horse carriage in the mud almost *ruptured* his guts and *pulled apart* his hips.[38] The weather in Beijing was unusually wet, and after a succession of rainy days, the muddy streets had become rutted under the crushing wheels of the cannons.

Cannons lay bogged down in the ruts. Soldiers were nowhere in sight, taking shelter who-knows-where from the rain, probably waiting for the rain to let up before moving the cannons. Hart marveled at the ease with which bold potential saboteurs could do their work. With a sigh, he said to himself, "How could the Chinese hope to achieve victory if this was the way they go to war?" When he mentioned his misgivings at the Zongli Yamen, the ministers replied that the public ought to be warned to keep away from the cannons. Hart shook his head. How were they to be warned? The soldiers should be ordered to stand by the cannons at all times!

But he knew nothing would come of his suggestions. Oh, he loved this country but found it exasperating at the same time. His mind suddenly went to his beloved son Bruce who also exasperated him. Campbell had written to Hart, saying that doctors in London were very concerned about Bruce's health. They advised consent to his marriage without delay, but also said that the wedding should be postponed in consideration of Bruce's heart condition. So Campbell proposed appointing Bruce as his personal secretary in the London office of the Chinese Customs.

At that point, China had lost the war and was at a critical moment. As mandated by the Chinese government, Hart busied himself with urging the British government to help as mediator and with purchasing arms. So concerning the situation with his son, he said only one word "Yes" in reply, on October 26—it covered everything: permission to be engaged, authority to pay debts, and appointment to the London Office.[39] Compared to the fate of China, his son's demands were too trivial to trouble his mind.

At the end of 1894, under the shadow of war, the imperial court refrained from the usual New Year celebrations. In early January, on the very day that China's envoy Zhang Yinhuan arrived in Japan, the important Chinese port of Weihai fell. What an ambience for the negotiations! A hardliner caucus was taking shape. Since the war was being fought on Chinese territory, the public was incensed. Zhang Yinhuan's mission ended in fiasco, and Li Hongzhang took over, with predictable results.

It was at this point that Bruce returned to China, bringing along his bride. This bad timing was somewhat symbolic. His son, the one person he loved most, the one on whom he had pinned high hopes, the one who exasperated and disappointed him, had come to China at a time of turbulence.

Toward the end of April 1895, Bruce and his wife arrived

at the Dagu Wharf. The young couple had married in defiance of Mrs. Hart, with whom they were hardly on speaking terms. But would they be able to get along with Hart? The bride was even more edgy than her husband. The hardships of the journey, the still smoldering ashes of the war, and the uncertainties of her future all took a toll on her health. Soon after she disembarked, she miscarried and had to be put up in a dismal-looking local inn. Hart sent Chen Afeng, his servant of 36 years, to Dagu to take care of Bruce and his bedridden young wife.

Two weeks later, they arrived in Beijing safe and sound.

On the day of their arrival, Hart happened to be free from official duties, something quite unusual for him. Since he had been the one who had almost ruined his daughter-in-law's marital prospects, he painstakingly prepared for a gift for her and racked his brains over ways to avoid awkwardness the first day they were to meet. The first thing to do was to change his preconceptions about his daughter-in-law, or at least to bury them in the depths of his heart.

He heard the bells of the horse-carriage. Then the carriage stopped and he heard them enter the compound. He remained seated in the host's chair in the reception room instead of going out to greet them—proper etiquette must be observed. The Chinese valued decorum as did the British. He suddenly realized that he had never been so tense even on the most important diplomatic occasions. Ah, domestic troubles were more exasperating than diplomatic problems!

The young couple came in and bowed deeply to him. They then sat down, took tea and exchanged pleasantries with him. His daughter-in-law came across as quite a nice young woman, quiet, composed and self-contained.

Father and son talked about family matters and about the journey while the daughter-in-law kept silent. Hart tried but failed to think up other topics to make her feel more at ease. Finally he brought up music, his own favorite subject. To his surprise, the young woman's face relaxed at this mention. She knew Mozart, Bach and Haydn, leading Hart to think, "She is very pleasant and her music is good, and she influences him for good."[40]

By this time, his former battle against his son's marriage seemed to him laughable and absurd. Hart's softening took a weight off Bruce's mind, and he began to work happily in his father's office. It was by no means an easy job. He had little knowledge of Chinese nor any work experience. With his weak constitution, he had recurrent bouts of ill health and depression. Deep down, Hart felt guilty about the way he had treated his son. The more he liked his daughter-in-law, the more he held himself responsible for the consequences of his harsh intervention in his son's marriage. In April 1896, Bruce had a heart attack, and in May, Hart decided to send him back to England. He even thought of abandoning his post and personally escorting his son back, writing to Campbell, "I am very grieved and very anxious! The doctor says there is the hope that if he keeps quiet he may grow out of it—but I am afraid of *heart failure*. Well—we all have our share of sorrow and joy, and nobody has a monopoly of either! I feel as if my life had been wasted—China, the country I served, in such a fix, and Bruce, the dear boy I worked for, in this distressing condition!"[41]

Chapter Nine

"I feel as if my life had been wasted." Those are the most unlikely words from Hart. For a man as self-assured and tenacious as he was, such a lament at over sixty years of age goes to show how much the situation with his son had distressed him

Of course, Bruce was not the only reason for that lament, although Hart's career was still going along well. On March 20, 1896, the Qing government appointed him as the I. G. of Customs and Posts. To establish a Chinese modern postal service had long been a dream of Hart's. Now that his endeavors had finally borne fruit, rather than rejoicing, he was lamenting a wasted life. Why? He was a man of vision, and even now in 1896, China remained far short of the modernity for which he had hoped. He was feeling old and worried that his strength was unequal to his ambition.

At age 62, Hart had become more realistic after having experienced more than forty years of the vicissitudes of life in China. Reform was not as simple as he had once thought. Twenty years ago, when handling the Margary case, he had set his mind on establishing a mint. But by 1896, he had changed his mind. "As for *Mints*, I am not so sure of my ground as I was twenty years ago: these Chinese in their continuous history of three thousand years of empire have gone through all sorts of experiences and experiments and have much to teach, and it strikes me they'd make a mistake were they to do away with *cash* and substitute cents and sixpences for as it is, they have the cheapest of metals—and the least variable—for their currency and every coin (cash) can buy something! To do away with this and substitute gold and silver will expose them to all the worry of the west and will raise prices tenfold in the ordinary life of the people I fear—and so I don't know now that I'd recommend Mints as means to power and pavement for the roads of progress!"[42]

He had lost his erstwhile vim and vigor. Profoundly disappointed in both Britain and China, he felt that only a major political upheaval in this dynasty could bring about vigorous reforms. But even though he knew that the Qing Dynasty's time must be drawing to an end, he saw nothing for it but to help it hang on. He felt duty-bound to perish with it.

To make matters worse, he had another problem on his hands: Bruce. It looked like Bruce had to cling to his father for support. He had never fully regained his health after his return to England, and his father was not entirely without blame for this. Bruce's London doctor said that there was in fact nothing wrong with his heart and that his ill health had been brought about by stress and worries.

Though father and son had never openly addressed the implication of that diagnosis, they were perfectly aware of it. Later, Bruce asked his father to buy him a house in Chislehurst in the suburbs of London, claiming that the doctor said a secluded place like that would be good for his health. Hart was not happy about the idea. Wouldn't it be better to find a small house in a cheaper neighborhood? He was no millionaire! But Bruce was dead set on making his father pay through the nose, as if seeking reparation. Hart complied in resignation.

These financial burdens meant that even if he had grown tired of the duties of the I. G., he had sufficient reason to wish to hold on to the job. He remained as hardworking as ever, and followed the same schedule he had for decades. He worked in his office, even on Sundays, from seven o'clock in the morning to 7:30 at night, with one break for lunch. It was the same, year in and year out.

But there was a difference from twenty or thirty years ago. He now felt it painful to work when one could see little hope. He wrote to Campbell, despairing, "The worst of it is I am utterly alone and have not a single friend or confidant— man, woman or child; of course occupation helps me, but, as I once before said, there come spasms of loneliness which hit hard."[43]

Those were turbulent years when there was no flicker of hope. He sensed this even among higher Chinese officials, some of whom even asked him to find out if he could get houses for them in Macao, as far from the capital as possible.[44] If Chinese high-level officials felt like that, what more could be expected of a foreigner?

Hart could only immerse himself in his work in order to fill the void in his heart and banish troubling thoughts from his mind. After establishing the Qing Imperial Postal Service, Hart planned to put all postal services under the management of the Customs. However since foreign legations had also established postal services of their own at some ports, Hart found it impossible to stop their operations. He came up with the idea of offering Custom discounts to foreign shipping companies that plied Chinese waters if they would carry mail only for the Qing Imperial Post and refuse all other mail. The foreign legations were furious, but Hart derived pleasure from these complications in his work.

In 1896, Bruce had a son, and the thought of his grandson brought brief solace to Hart. The year-end festivities also lifted his spirit, but tribulations continued to plague him.

Reform was brewing from 1897 to 1898, but Hart watched the developments with an impassive eye.

On January 1, 1898, Hart appointed Robert Bredon, his

brother-in-law, as Deputy I. G., the first time this post had been used in the history of the Chinese Customs. He had not appointed a deputy I. G. until now, most probably because he didn't want his power to fall into other people's hands. He trusted only his own kin. He had once named his brother as a successor but, to his regret, James Hart was not interested, and that attempt to launch him on a career had ultimately not worked out. Now that he had his brother-in-law onboard, Hart brought the Zongli Yamen around to the idea, and began preparations for his withdrawal from the frontlines.

The solar eclipse of January 22, 1898 turned out to be a bad omen. At dusk in Beijing, the mostly eclipsed sun looked like a new moon. In China, such celestial phenomena often led to fear and despair, especially in times of turmoil. And indeed, troubled times lay ahead.

Following the killing of two German missionaries on November 11, 1897, which became known as the Juye Incident, Germany sent warships to seize Jiaozhou Bay. In March 1898, the Qing court was coerced into leasing Jiaozhou Bay to Germany as a military port, allowing Germany to build railways, and opening up mines in Shandong. Thereafter, Russia, France and Britain followed suit in a wave of territorial demands.

The imperialist powers' intensified scramble for Chinese territory fanned the fire of reform all over China. Some new measures unimaginable in the past had now become possible. After November 1897, Emperor Guangxu's tutor Weng Tonghe approached Hart quite a few times to explore the possibility of working together to put Hart's reform ideas into operation. But Hart was filled with conflicting thoughts. At his age, he was no longer the energetic man he had been, and there was no predicting what twists and turns of the road lay ahead. He had seen too much, and felt that it was the fearless young who could accomplish great deeds in this world.

After turning the matter over and over in his mind, Hart reached a compromise with himself. He no longer had the inclination to set lofty goals and vigorously act on them. He also no longer held onto the idea of quitting and returning to his home country to live out his life in retirement. Committed to life in China, he asked Campbell to buy for him daily necessities and gifts, and prepared to render his home in China more comfortable in his declining years. He bought a house in Beidaihe, a summer resort near Beijing, and, handing over the daily work at the Customs to the newly promoted Deputy I. G., went to Beidaihe to enjoy his vacation.

In the summer of 1898 some momentous events were to take place. With help from Kang Youwei, the noted scholar and political reformer, and others, Emperor Guangxu had launched reforms efforts, but these were aborted after just 103 days under the intervention of Empress Dowager Cixi, leading this period to be known as the Hundred-Day Reform. Cixi staged a coup d'état and put Guangxu under house arrest.

It was on June 11, 1898, that Emperor Guangxu issued the first of the reform decrees, and it was June 11, 1898, that Hart left Beijing for Beidaihe on vacation. It was on September 21 that Cixi put Guangxu under house arrest, and it was September 21 that Hart returned to Beijing. Not a day too early or too late—he had managed to keep himself completely clear of these events!

Hart had never before gone off on vacation by himself in China, and had always kept a close eye on Customs business even when he was on home leave in Britain. This was the first time he had completely freed himself from all work, to every appearance as if he had deliberately avoided the turmoil. But even if Hart had accidentally acquired information about the starting date of Guangxu's reform, he could absolutely not have known that after 103 days, the Empress Dowager would make her move against the Emperor. And, even if Hart, with his immense almost magical powers, had kept Cixi's every move under surveillance, it would not have been possible for him, given the state of communication and transportation technology, to rush back to Beijing the very same day he received the news.

It had to be a coincidence.

By this mysterious coincidence, he had managed to avoid becoming entangled during these soul-stirring 103 days, and to good effect, for himself and for China. The fact was that Cixi liked Hart. But by 1898, Hart had clearly taken Guangxu's side in his political stance. Had he been in Beijing, would he have been involved in the Hundred-Day Reform to some degree? It was highly likely. The mysterious hand of fate had been at work, keeping Hart from losing Cixi's good graces. And so he found himself in the pivotal role of a mediator in the negotiations between the Qing Court and the eight-power allied forces two years later.

But in 1898, upon returning to Beijing from Beidaihe, Hart found, to his bewilderment, that the upper echelons of the court had been put into chaos during his brief absence. The Empress Dowager Cixi had pushed the Emperor into the shadows, and she emerged from backstage to openly assume the reins of the government. With a sinking feeling, he realized that there was not going to be any reform any time soon.

The Empress Dowager Cixi forged ahead ruthlessly and calmly. In spite of her advanced age, she was surprisingly capable and persevering. She had everything under her control. No one knew the Emperor's whereabouts or what had happened to him.

Hart found himself off the central stage but never stopped analyzing the political situation. He could, however, do no more than deduce and guess from appearances, which was why his judgments and his emotions kept undergoing changes, at times despairing and at others appearing hopeful. But by December 11, he was firmly pessimistic again, noting "Everything looks gloomy: the Empress Dow is hurrying on military preparations everywhere: and I fear we are far from the end of trouble."

Hart spent the rest of the year 1898 in trepidation.

In 1898, while foreign powers were vying for dominancy in China, the British government secured a promise from the Qing government that the Inspector General of the Customs would always be British. The Zongli Yamen gave in to this demand mainly because of Hart's outstanding performance, apart from the need for continuity. In balancing the interests of Britain and China and those of the other powers, Hart kept the ship of the Chinese Customs on a steady course with his remarkable political skills. This was not a post that could be easily filled by just anyone.

But by the end of the 19th century, Britain's status was no longer what it had been half a century earlier. It had lost its dominance in the military and economic arenas, and had been reduced to being just *one* of the world powers. So it would have been wise for Britain to have quietly kept the status quo. Once Hart retired, a replacement in Britain would have been found, with no one any the wiser. It all should have been kept quiet. And yet the foolish British Minister did exactly the opposite and went public, thinking he had won a victory.

This put Hart on the spot, and he was afraid of the consequences, wondering if now each power would appropriate a certain port and tell the Yamen that the Commissioner there must always be one of their nationals.[45] Sure enough, in February of 1899, Japan demanded the appointment of a Japanese Commissioner for the Xiamen [Amoy] Customs and, before long, the United States and Russia demanded an increase of their nationals in the Chinese Customs. Hart was greatly upset that the foreign powers' rivalry in China had extended to his turf.

At the end of February, the Italian Minister demanded from the Zongli Yamen the right to lease Sanmen Bay on the coast of Zhejiang as a coaling station and a navy base. Not one to lag behind in this competition, Britain now wanted its sphere of influence in Hong Kong to be expanded to Kowloon. The good Sino-British relationship that Hart had built up through decades of hard work would be destroyed at one stroke and, as a consequence, his political footing crumbling. He asked for permission to take a long vacation but the Zongli Yamen denied the request. He was desperate to go away. It was out of character for him to do so, but he had no alternative. While feeling helpless, he also sensed *a curious feeling of unrest among the Chinese just now and they seem to expect something serious to occur this summer.*[46]

From July 1 to September 21, he stayed at Beidaihe. The vacation without interference from work only made him feel worse, just as had been the case when he was on his home leave many years before. Once back in Beijing, he found that no one in the Zongli Yamen seemed to be engaged in anything except worry. The weather had been dry for a long time in Beijing. With Heaven turning a deaf ear to prayers for rain, the Emperor repeatedly issued decrees, demanding everyone to exercise caution in word and in deed. There was also anxiety about the plague that had claimed the lives of several Russians in Niuzhuang although it had not yet spread to Beijing.

It was a time of crises in daytime and festivities at night. Despair and hope, agony and pleasure mixed together until it was hard to tell the true from the false.

Hart was pessimistic about the situation: "Here everything is, as it were, dead: there is no vitality and no growth—China is hibernating. People see that change is wanted, but the whole huge edifice is so rickety, that, although it will stand for years if left alone, the fear is that the moving of one brick may bring down the structure."[47]

By November, winter had arrived in full force, the trees stripped of all leaves. While celebrations for the Empress Dowager's birthday were going on in Beijing, the plague was in full swing in Niuzhuang, diarrhea was prevalent in Tianjin, and malaria was ravaging other places. The Zongli Yamen was busy addressing financial problems—paying dividends on bonds and raising funds for the army.

During the 1900 New Year celebrations, Hart in Beijing got word about the Boxer Rebellion, but he was not yet aware that the rebellion was to change the fate of China.

Hart had stayed indoors since before Christmas. He had caught a cold and then he was afflicted with lumbago. He felt he had grown old, his *youth gone completely!*[48]

By March, word came of the union of the Boxers, so-called due to their origins in the secret Society of Righteous and Harmonious Fists, and government officials. On April 6, the ministers of Britain, the US, Germany and France sent the Zongli Yamen a demand that the Qing government wipe out the Boxers within two months.

There were divisions of opinion and strategy, both within the Chinese leadership and the foreign powers, and the situation continued to worsen. Toward the end of May, the Qing government issued three harshly worded decrees, demanding the immediate arrest of the ringleaders and the dispersal of the Boxers, but things remained out of control. In reality, the highest authorities did not really mean to keep the situation under control. So under the pretext of protecting the legations, the Powers dispatched troops into the Beijing and Tianjin region, heightening tension.

Judging from the information gathered by the Customs, Hart also felt threatened by the Boxers. He saw a crisis coming. There were rumors that the Empress Dowager herself had been brought around to the side of the Boxers, and he was not sure about other top Chinese leaders' real position. He had no access to inside information. While the Zongli Yamen assured him that he was safe, he felt that anything could happen any time now.

Hart was seized with fear. His past letters to Campbell were written in the tone of a Chinese government official but now he had switched to the side of the foreigners, assessing the situation from that perspective. In fact this was quite natural.

The Boxers were xenophobic, and the Qing government was in fact on the Boxers' side at that moment. Even though he was an official appointed by the Chinese court, he would not be able to stay immune from the ravages of the storm, and things did turn out the way he had feared.

On May 27, after several days' reflection, Hart wrote, "The Court appears to be in a dilemma: if the Boxers are not suppressed the Legations threaten to take action—if the attempt to suppress them is made, this intensely patriotic organization will be converted into an anti-dynastic movement! Que faire? The fact that this year has an eighth intercalary moon prepares the Chinese mind not only to expect, but to help along untoward occurrences. We have been crying 'Wolf' all the last fifty years and still life goes on as before, but some day or other there is bound to be a cataclysm."

On June 10, Hart telegraphed Campbell, telling him that the future looked gloomy, that Christians were the only ones not sympathizing with the Boxers, that the Legation Quarter was packed with priests taking refuge, and that the Boxers had gradually moved into the city proper.

There was not a sound to be heard. Not even pigeon whistles. Even the pigeons had stopped flying.

Beijing is beautiful in June, the first month of summer. Freed from the sandstorms of spring, its air smells sweet with new foliage, grass and flowers. This was the season for horse-riding and pleasure outings to the suburbs and picnics. The foreign community in Beijing had always bustled with one party after another in June of earlier years, and the Customs' brass band had always been fully booked. Nothing gave Hart more joy than to see his band rush to one performance after another. It was the only brass band in Beijing and in China at the time.

But June this year saw nothing of the kind.

Hart was in no mood to work, nor would it have been possible for him to work if he wanted to. The Chinese government and people were up against the entire Western world. He was a Westerner employed by the Chinese government, with a group of Westerners under him, dealing with Western merchants. How was this to be done? Hart had never been baffled by anything until now. Not only did he find it impossible to conduct his work, he had no idea how bad things might become. He had fought all his life for China to learn from the West and develop as the West had done. All his decades-long efforts had now gone down the drain.

He was not concerned about his personal safety. His family was not there and he was an old man. He felt no fear but only grief in his spacious but quite empty room.

All of a sudden, there was a noise—cries of human voices as powerful as the roar of ocean tides. Hart's house was located on the periphery of the Legation Quarter and, therefore, on the first line of defense of the foreign troops. Beyond the fortifications of sandbags gathered an ever swelling crowd of Boxers—thousands upon thousands of them—whose heavy breathing alone had merged into a low pitched roar.

The temporary guards coming from the various legations were too few in number to be spread out effectively over a long battle line. They had to shorten the line and await reinforcements. On June 13, this outer defense line was abandoned and the Boxers swarmed over like a wave. Hart's house caught fire. Without stopping to take his clothes or other necessities, he fled to the British Legation.

On June 20, the Qing court decided after a heated debate to declare war on the foreign powers, with troops laying siege to the Legation Quarter in Beijing. All contacts with the outside were severed. Probably because Hart's house was burned down and no news about him had been heard, rumors began to circulate in Britain that he had been killed by the Boxers. On July 17, *The Times* even carried his obituary! The British government planned to hold a memorial service for him and abandoned the idea only because of Campbell's objections.

Luckily no memorial service was held, because Hart was very much alive, holed up in the British Legation with other foreign nationals for 58 days. During that time he never stopped trying to maintain contact with the Zongli Yamen, from which he received a note on July 21, saying that F. E. Taylor, the statistical secretary at the Shanghai Customs, had been appointed to assume temporary direction of the Customs. Hart asked the Zongli Yamen to send a telegram on his behalf to Aglen, Commissioner of Customs in Shanghai, saying, "Happily still alive! I have authorised yourself and Taylor carry on Inspector General's work. Observe utmost economy, and wire Yamen when in difficulty. Direct communication impossible, and weather, etc., make it hot for all here."[49]

During the siege, Hart remained calm and often told jokes to put the others at ease. For the first time in a long while, he had the leisure to do things that he had always wanted to do but had never had time. In the midst of the fear and alarm, he began calmly writing a series of articles. The first was on the current situation, "The Peking Legations: A National Uprising and International Episode," which was published in the November 1900 issue of *The Fortnightly Review.*

He sat in the Legation, listening to the gunfire and racket outside, with Chinese troops and rebels about to charge in any time to kill him. And he, a so-called British devil, was not focused on his own safety but rather on his adopted country. A flood of memories of his 46 years in China overtook him. Thinking back he realized that all the years he had spent in China had been worthwhile. Having only recently escaped from the Boxers bent on killing him, he picked up a pencil and, ignoring any likely recriminations from public opinion in the West, including his home country, began to defend China and the Boxer Rebellion rationally and courageously:

"This episode of to-day is not meaningless—it is the prelude to a century of change and the keynote of the future history of the Far East: the China of the year 2000 will be very different from the China of 1900! National sentiment is a constant factor which must be recognized, and not eliminated when dealing with national facts, and the one feeling that is universal in China is pride in Chinese institutions and contempt for foreign: treaty intercourse has not altered this—if anything, it has deepened it, and the future will not be uninfluenced by it."[50]

With regard to the idea of a partition of China, he wrote, "With such an enormous population, it could never be expected to be a final settlement, and unrest and unhappiness and uncertainty would run through all succeeding generations. The Chinaman is a very practical person, and accepts the rule of those who have the power to rule and the good sense to rule justly with greater equanimity than others; but, all the same, there is such a thing as Chinese feeling and Chinese aspiration, and those will never be stamped out, but will live and seethe and work beneath the surface through all time, even under the most beneficent rule, and in the end—it may be sooner, it may be later—assert themselves and win their object. ... [This is] as certain as that the sun will shine tomorrow."[51]

The German Kaiser Wilhelm II had said that China would rise in the 20th century and, once risen, China would follow the footsteps of the wide-conquering Mongol Empire. To his claim that a partition of China was the only way to forestall another "Yellow Peril," Hart had this rebuttal: "The Chinese, an intelligent, cultivated race, sober, industrious, and on its own lines civilized, homogeneous in language, thought, and feeling, which numbers some four hundred millions, lives in its own ring-fence, and covers a country made up of fertile land and teeming waters, with infinite variety of mountain and of plain, hill and dale, and every kind of climate and condition, producing on its surface all that a people requires and hiding in its bosom untold virgin wealth that has never yet been disturbed—this race, after thousands of years of haughty seclusion and exclusiveness, has been pushed by the force of circumstances and by the superior strength of assailants into treaty relations with the rest of the world, but regards that as a humiliation, sees no benefit accruing from it, and is looking forward to the day when it in turn will be strong enough to revert to its old life again and do away with foreign intercourse, interference, and intrusion."[52]

Hart defended the justice of the Boxers' cause as a purely patriotic volunteer movement, with an objective to strengthen China, and at the conclusion of the article, wrote, "What has happened has been the logical effect of previous doings. Europe ... has wounded her: a more tactful, reasonable, and consistent course might possibly have produced better results, but in no case could foreigners expect to maintain for ever their extra-territorialized status and the various commercial stipulations China had conceded to force. As to the future, it must be confessed that Chinese, so far, have not shone as soldiers: but there are brave men among them and their number will increase; if the China of to-day did not hesitate on the 19th June to throw down the glove to a dozen Treaty Powers, is the China of a hundred years hence less likely to do so? Of course common sense may keep China from initiating an aggressive policy and from going to extremes; but foreign dictation must some day cease and foreigners some day go, and the episode now called attention to is to-day's hint to the future."[53]

On August 3 and August 5, Hart sent two short letters respectively to Shanghai: The first one expressed hope to be freed from the difficulties as soon as possible, and the second one asked for autumn and winter clothes because everything had been burned up.

Finally, on August 14, the eight-power allied forces advanced into Beijing. At four o'clock that afternoon, Grand Secretary Gang Yi entered the palace and reported to the Empress Dowager Cixi that the foreign troops were already in Beijing. He pleaded for the Empress Dowager and the Emperor to leave the city. At midnight, a Grand Council meeting was held. And four o'clock the next morning, Cixi, for the first time in her life, combed her hair in a Han-Chinese style rather than one of her Manchu ancestry, and disguised as a peasant woman, secretly left the palace in an ordinary sedan-chair. She met the princes and the ministers at Yuanmingyuan and fled to Xi'an.

The man sat in a teak chair facing the open bedroom door, within view of the corridor that led to the inner courtyard. He was in full court regalia, complete with his hat. In his left hand was a foldable fan and in his right hand, a gleaming razor. His beautifully embroidered robe was splashed all over with the blood of the two women on the bed behind him. Both women's throats had been cut, but their tracheas not cleanly cut through. They were still convulsing, blood still flowed. A boy not yet able to walk was lying, alive, on his stomach by them. The man did not have the courage to kill his son.

The man was waving his fan to drive away the flies attracted by the smell of blood in the hot weather. He was calmly waiting for the foreign soldiers. When gun-toting foreigners eventually showed up, finding their way through the outer courtyard, the man raised his right hand and with a smile gently slit his own throat. His blood spurted like a red fountain. The three foreign soldiers, who had been in high spirits, were dumbfounded. As they recoiled, the razor fell with a clang from the man's hand onto the floor while the fan in his left hand was still shaking.

Many other men and women of the Manchu aristocracy committed suicide, and thousands upon thousands of people were killed by the occupying eight-power allied troops on a killing spree.

The city of Beijing had been looted and pillaged before, first by the Boxer Rebels and then by Qing soldiers out of control. But both times, only the top layer of the fat was skimmed off. Now the foreign soldiers were at it brutally but systematically.

They began with random lootings, spreading themselves out throughout the city. Then each contingent looted the areas whose security it had been mandated to safeguard. In the last stage, the commanders established cache spots for looted goods in an attempt to make a show of establishing order out of the chaos, and ordered that all looted goods be surrendered to appointed caretakers. Only the Japanese soldiers complied. Soldiers of the Western powers paid no heed to the directive. Treating all the people of Beijing and their property as bounty for the taking, the soldiers plunged into beastly atrocities.

Once assured of his personal safety, Hart telegraphed Campbell and instructed him: "Send quickly two autumn office suits and later two winter ditto with morning and evening dress, warm cape, and four pairs of boots and slippers."[54] He had set to work again.

Hart was the kind of person with a strong sense of mission and an urge to excel. The greater the challenge, the greater his fighting spirit. Beijing was in chaos, a city without leaders, without government. The eight-power allied troops were a loosely put together force, each nation with its own interests. Their internal clashes were certain to intensify, and with winter soon to be upon them, the expeditionary forces would run into more problems. It was not that easy to carve up China. There was urgent need for someone to step in and mediate between China and the Western powers to solve the crisis. None but Hart fit that role.

Rendered homeless, he had taken up quarters in two rooms behind a shop owned by Mr. Kierulff, husband of his onetime housekeeper. The rooms also doubled as his office. No sooner had he moved in than he set to work.

On September 8, he picked up a pencil and wrote his first letter to Campbell about the earthshaking changes and his worries about how he could be of use in the difficult negotiations. At the same time, he continued to write for Western journals. His article "China and Her Foreign Trade" was sent to *North American Review,* and his article "China and Reconstruction," a firm rebuttal of the idea of a partition of China, was published in the January issue of *The Fortnightly Review.*

Hart firmly opposed high-handed measures against China, and worried about the effects that delays in negotiations were having on trade and revenue across the country. In an article, "China and Non-China" written in November 1900 and published in the February 1901 issue of *The Fortnightly Review,* he cited examples to illustrate his point that misunderstandings stemmed from different cultural perspectives. Hart believed that Westerners' understanding of the Chinese was too shallow, and to give a good prescription for China's longstanding afflictions, they must understand the Chinese nation. He pointed out, "They [the Chinese] are well-behaved, law-abiding, intelligent, economical, and industrious,—they can learn anything and do anything, — they are punctiliously polite, they worship talent, and they believe in right so firmly that they scorn to think it requires to be supported or enforced by might,—they delight in literature, and everywhere they have their literary clubs and coteries for hearing and discussing each other's essays and verses, —they possess and practise an admirable system of ethics, and they are generous, charitable, and fond of good works, —they never forget a favour, they make rich return for any kindness, and, though they know money will buy service, a man must be more than wealthy to win public esteem and respect."[55]

Another article "The Boxers: 1900," written in December 1900 and published in the March 1901 issue of *Deutsche Revue,* was an expansion of the previous article. These articles, which were later compiled into a pamphlet titled *These from the Land of Sinim,* contain ideas that have basically been proven correct over the last hundred years. But it was precisely because he was ahead of his time that his articles generated strong negative reactions outside of China. His views had never been heard of in the West and were completely unacceptable to the majority of readers.

Hart was not afraid of criticism. He wrote to Campbell, "I can imagine all the hard things it [his article] would tempt smart critics to fire off ...: but, all the same, the fact will remain that China will go on along a new road to gather strength and that foreign invasion will be met in another way next time. ... The four papers I have written are linked together and have an object, and that is to endeavor to create a better feeling and better relations between China and non-China: but, of course, other people will hold other views and on such a big question there must be great variety of opinion."[56]

Hart's series of articles had strong repercussions. The issue of *The Fortnightly Review* carrying his "China's Reconstruction" ran seven reprints within one month and had a major impact on the political situation. With his prestige in Western countries as a China hand, his ideas of preserving rather than partitioning China were finally accepted after much debate. His ideas put to rest the in-fighting among the imperialist powers and led to plans acceptable to them as well as to the Chinese government. Even Wilhelm II of Germany, who had coined the phrase "Yellow Peril," acknowledged that carving up China was unrealistic.

But writing articles did not suffice to solve problems. Hart had his plate full as a mediator.

Winter was soon upon Beijing. Hart had never experienced such a harsh winter in China. His temporary quarters had no heating facilities. It was bitterly cold and the supplies sent from London had not yet arrived. With only one change of clothes, he sometimes had to work in bed, under his quilt. The I. G. had never before cut such a sorry figure.

He had heavy responsibilities on his shoulders. He began to consult Prince Qing and Li Hongzhang, but the Russian Minister was away, the German Minister had not yet taken up his post, the British Minister was leaving, and the French Minister was confined to his bed with typhoid fever. Hart's mission as a mediator was beset with difficulties. However he was busier than ever. He hoped to finish the preparational stage and delve into substantial negotiations as soon as possible.

Hart's arguments were not the only, or even the main, reason for the termination of the partition of China by the eight Powers. It would have been truly difficult to persuade any invader to give up the goodies he had already laid his hands on. The deciding factor was that almost at the same time the allied forces were advancing into Beijing, a 200,000-strong Russian army was taking the whole of Manchuria. The conflicts among the Powers intensified. In order to maintain a balance among their national interests, they preferred to maintain the status quo in the China. And so it was for their own interests that they opted for a compromise.

Hart's working conditions were harsh. For a 65-year-old man, it was a daunting challenge to resume the operations of the Customs Service and start afresh.

Hart's age had taken a toll on his memory. He had long been working on the basis of his notes and memos. And now, he worried, "My memory has nothing in it, and I am very much at a loss about all sorts of things, public and private; the loss of my official archives and private papers etc. has been, and will be, terrible calamity of Service and self—but there it is, and crying won't help spilt milk! The future is perplexing."[57] How was the Customs Service to survive? He hoped that China would still be left to enjoy administrative integrity so that the I. G. would remain an important figure and *a bigger man in the future than in the past.*[58]

Hart was understandably anxious about the fate of the Chinese Customs, to which he had devoted a lifetime of service. Toward the end of December, he began to see light at the end of the tunnel. Negotiations on the Customs Service began. Representatives of foreign powers reached consensus and signed the jointly drafted documents. No changes were introduced to Hart's Customs.

With mixed feelings, he wrote to Campbell, "I wish I were ten years younger as I should like to have the handling of affairs for another decade, but I fear another year is as much as I shall have left to devote to China—however I fancy I can put through much that will be important and start the chariot of progress on the wheels of the future. As I write I feel there is a lull in the excited atmosphere of the place: it is Xmas Eve and all are preparing for Xmas Day. I am, so to speak, homeless, and alone, and all I can do is to take a cold bath of a mind-strengthening kind in the cold waters of philosophy: all the merriment of the season, as far as I am concerned, lies in recollection, and if I am not tremendously jolly this year I can at all events relive many fairly enjoyable times that have sunk in the waters of the past. The great thing is that my health holds out, but sundry twitchings at various points startle me occasionally and I daresay I shall yet have a breakdown to face: I hope it will hold off till I have done my part towards putting things in order once more. I have had many a bitter dose to swallow, but I always say 'never mind—the sun will shine tomorrow and the tortoise may again beat the hare!'"[59]

In the summer of 1901, Hart did not go on vacation to Beidaihe. His house there had been burned down by the Boxers. He remained working in Beijing, contented by having maintained and increased the influence of the Customs. He ordered musical instruments and pieces of music from England in a bid to put together his band again. He also bought a set of the *Oxford Pocket Classics* in two cases, the Greek in one, the Latin in the other. This meant that he was planning to stay on in China. He was in good spirits.

While the badly burned Customs building and his own residence were under reconstruction, he asked Campbell to buy furniture and all other necessary items from London. Because the white oak dining table for eighteen persons he had specified was not available, Campbell had one made by H. M. Office of Works. His desk was also made to look like the one in a photograph of his. In early September, eight sets of bedroom furniture, a dining set including the custom-made dining table, a mirror, chairs, china cabinet and fully equipped billiard table as well as furniture for his study, his office and his reception room were all shipped. Other items like silverware, musical instruments, carpets, mirrors, curtains and cleaning items were still being bought.

All seemed to be going well, although his younger brother James in England came down with neurosis after long years of excessive drinking, and his son Bruce also had a nervous breakdown. This was hard on Hart as he was trying to pull everything together.

The rebuilding was still going on and he thought he would be in the house by the Chinese New Year. Unfortunately his own health began to take a turn for the worse. He wished to go back to see his home country and friends—the few that were left—once more. This would have to wait, however, until after the Indemnity arrangements were completed, the Native Customs transfer put through, and the Custom re-organization provided for.[60]

In acknowledgment of Hart's contribution in the peace talks, the Chinese imperial court granted him the title of Junior Guardian of the Heir Apparent, a title that had just been bestowed on Zhang Zhidong and Yuan Shikai. It would have been previously unthinkable for a foreigner to acquire such a great honor.

Due to delays in the rebuilding project, Hart was not able to relocate before the Chinese New Year. The winter of 1901 was bitterly cold. He had a bad cough and there was no regular heating. It might not have been a problem for young man, but Hart was getting on in years.

Chapter Ten

The invasion of the allied forces in 1900 was a great shock to the Qing Dynasty rulers. Cixi began to reform, annulling the traditional-format civil service exams and the old military exams, encouraging studies abroad, restructuring the military, training troops using Western methods, advocating and rewarding private enterprises, allowing intermarriage between Han Chinese and Manchus, and prohibiting the binding of women's feet. These were all changes that Hart had hoped for, changes that had been long overdue.

In his declining years, Hart remained important to the Chinese Customs and to the Qing government. Though many people, including himself, hated the idea of his departure, everyone knew that eventually he would have to go, and that day was not too far off. In addition to doing his daily work, he began to make arrangements for the future.

His ill health was a constant reminder of that necessity. The constant flare-ups of lumbago made him worry: "Being now well on to '70,' the machinery—which has worked so well through so many years—is naturally wearing thin: so a collapse may come any day. The only thing that gives me any worry—unfinished work and family griefs apart—is the existence of so many volumes of my Journal: I now wish it had gone to the flames with my other belongings."[61]

Hart had wanted to re-read the diaries accumulated over so many years but he found himself unequal to the task. He just burned the part about Ayao in his earlier entries, and this alone took up much of his time. Other parts of the diaries also contained things he did not want to be seen, but they were so deeply embedded in valuable historical records that it would take too much work to carefully sieve and discard them. He had never anticipated this dilemma when making those entries, and he couldn't brace himself for committing them to flames. He instructed Campbell, "If I die out here, and have time to do so, I'll tell people to send it [the journal] to you, and you can make it over to Bruce to keep as a family curio—and not to be either published or lent to writers of any kind: note this, please—'R.I.P!'"[62]

In April 1902, Hart's house was ready. It looked from the outside very much like its old self, only slightly taller. But to Hart, it was a totally different, large and empty house with no reminders of his life accumulated day after day over the years.

After his lumbago went away, he began to be assailed by severe headaches, which could last from his rise from bed to about ten o'clock in the morning. Sometimes, the left posterior lobe of the brain hurt badly, accompanied by a stiffness that seemed to spread down from the left side of his neck and shoulder. He was worried that this could be a sign of paralysis.

The rebuilt house still needed to be aired out before it could be occupied. When the furniture was unpacked, he found it not as good as what had come from London before, complaining that "the desk and the pigeonholes don't compare with the lost ones and Wright's Billiard Table and accessories are very shabby after Thurston!"[63] In spite of all these disappointments, he was still happy to move into the new house, to be under his own roof once more.

He returned to his rebuilt house on May 26. Finally he had a peaceful home of his own on the original site. He toured all the rooms. Another person would have found everything the same as before, but in his eyes, everything was a poor replica of its original, as if made to mock him. Of course one has to say goodbye to one's past life at some point, and he was just doing it a little in advance. In fact, was it even necessary to replicate his past? He had only a couple more years ahead of him, and would only be there for a short time before returning home. Soon he would be bidding farewell to his past.

When working or resting or sleeping in his new house, he would often wonder in what way would death come to him. Maybe in a way he had never even thought of. Then he would think that he must be getting old if he was worrying about dropping dead any minute. Luckily for him, he was too busy with work to indulge in much self pity.

On November 13, 1902, Hart's younger brother James died of gastric hemorrhage in Brighton. It grieved Hart that he had not been able to meet James alive once more. But at least his years away had been worth it—China was advancing in the direction he had always hoped.

By 1903, Hart had been the I. G. for forty straight years. He was a true autocrat, with unmonitored, centralized power. Even the most competent, brilliant and ethical person cannot be immune from flaws. And even if there had been no major failings, forty years of minor imperfections add up and give rise to frictions and clashes in the workplace. When it looked as if the tempting post of I. G. was finally about to open up, now that old age and infirmity had settled upon Hart, was it any surprise that all was not quiet in the Customs Service?

The naming of a successor to Robert Hart was the talk of the town. Robert Bredon, his brother-in-law, was of mediocre ability. Hart's insistence that Bredon be his successor drew much criticism. Campbell felt the need to report to Hart what he had heard, also using this as a way of mildly expressing his own view. But these words fell on the obstinate Hart's profoundly deaf ears.

His house in Beidaihe had been rebuilt. He went there again on vacation, but he fainted when he was about to return to Beijing. This had never happened before. He was a little nervous as was his family. After all, he was almost seventy, living all alone on the other side of the ocean, without a family member to take care of him. Mrs. Hart decided to pay him a visit. The Siberian Railway had already been built, so Europeans could now take the train to China rather than the much longer route by sea. Since some spots along the railway route were not safe, Mrs. Hart decided to instead travel to China with their daughter by sea. However with a war looming between Russia and Japan, a sea route would not be safe, either. In the end, they decided to postpone the visit to the spring of 1904.

Hart began to make arrangements for the future, compiling a list of his investments and assets for Campbell, and giving his last will and testament to the Hutchins' law office.

The long anticipated Russo-Japanese War broke out on February 6, 1904. It was fought on Chinese territory and therefore had an enormous impact on China.

Then in late spring and early summer of 1904, British troops invaded Tibet, meeting with brave resistance from Tibetan troops at Jiangzi. Had this happened ten years earlier, Hart would surely have been involved in a mediating role, however painful it might be to him. But he was old now and the job of a mediator was beyond him, nor did the Qing government expect him to take it on. He was strictly a neutral observer just as he was during the Russo-Japanese War, which ended in Japanese victory.

Hart languished in ill health. The question of his succession remained outstanding. He still wanted his brother-in-law Robert Bredon to take over but, deep down, he was not very satisfied with his own choice. Bredon often clashed with his colleagues and all too clearly lacked the magnanimity of mind and the interpersonal skills necessary for such an important post. The British Foreign Office did not approve of the candidate, and the Chinese government that held Hart in such respect remained ambivalent. But Hart held his ground.

Hart asked the Zongli Yamen for permission to take home leave. In a written reply, the Zongli Yamen stated that while they understood his request, he was quite indispensable, and Hart felt obliged to withdraw his request.

Robert Bredon arrived in Beijing from Shanghai. Six or seven years earlier, Hart had promised that if he went on leave or retired, he would recommend Bredon to the Zongli Yamen to act for or succeed him. Bredon was confident that he would have the support of all the Chinese officials, most of the Customs staff, and many foreign legations. If the British Foreign Office opposed, he would defend what he held to be his rights.

Hart knew that the situation was not as Bredon had imagined. To avoid a conflict, the Chinese government wanted Hart to stay on but if Hart did, Bredon would not like it, and the issue of succession would only be shelved rather than resolved. In this dilemma, Hart decided on a temporary strategy: "I shall only touch big questions and I'll put every bit of work I can on his shoulders: then, in spring, I'll try to go on leave for some months, and perhaps the storm will keep off and even the threatening clouds be dispersed."[64]

With Hart transferring much of the work to him, Bredon gradually set his mind at rest. But Prince Qing had not yet declared himself. He only passed on a message to Hart from the imperial court that he should stay put and not raise the succession question by going away. But Hart desperately wanted to get away: "Even if I stay on, my health or death may raise the trouble any day. My nature desire for rest, change, and a visit home is increased, too, by the feeling that C'toms work grows heavier and more difficult, and wants a younger and more active man: I have done my fair share—I have kept things together, formed the Service, broadened its basis, hardened its foundation, and made a fine position for any other man to climb higher from, and I ought to be let go. But there is no denying of it, the Chinese Govt. will have a difficulty when I move, and I have prepared them for this years ago—but they have done nothing towards getting ready to meet it, and, in fact, nothing would prepare them to meet it except such development in strength as would enable them to take their own course without fear—but that course would then probably be the wiping out of the foreign element![65]

The Chinese New Year came around. On the morning of the first day of the first lunar month, all the Chinese employees of the lower levels of the Customs, about 200 of them, went to offer their New Year greetings to Hart. On the fifth of the month, Prince Qing had lunch with him. On the eleventh day of the same month, the Empress Dowager summoned Hart for an audience and said to him, "You are now acclimatized to China and you had better stay where you are!" That very same day, he had dinner with Prince Pulun. The Chinese government was showering him with honors, hoping he would stay in his post.

Hart felt that his life was coming to an end. When a man is at that stage of his life, he needs to bring closure to things that he has not been able to tackle. Of course there may be things that are never settled. In Hart's case, the fruits of his de facto marriage in his youth were still there. Even though he had made meticulous arrangements from early on, he never acknowledged his fatherhood and had even sent his two sons Herbert and Arthur to the remotest part of the British Commonwealth—Canada. Yet they remained his sons.

Something happened in the autumn of 1905. It was a case of blackmail. It did not amount to much, but it did add anxieties to Hart's already vexed mind.

When Hart was about to end his career in China, his wife arrived for a visit. She had not visited China since 1882, and they had been living apart for 23 years. Countless times Hart had wanted to go to England on home leave but had never made it for one reason or another. His wife, however, could have come any time. It was understandable that she felt uncomfortable living in China on a long-term basis but she could have paid some visits—every five years or even every ten. But, for 23 years she stayed away. Did they still qualify as husband and wife? The debt was heavily in his favor. If she were to stay away longer, she would have been deprived of a chance of paying it back.

Goodness knows how many times Hart looked forward to a visit from his wife, but the desire had cooled off by now. This visit was actually more for her sake than for his. It was to ease her guilty conscience. Hart would be hard put to refuse her visit but did express his irritation in a letter to Campbell, especially about the fact that he would have to go out into society when she was around.[66]

On March 2, 1906, Mrs. Hart arrived in Beijing with their younger daughter. At the entrance to his residence, Hart embraced his daughter and, after a slight hesitation, he put his arms around his wife. When they touched, he felt his own muscles tighten. He sensed that his wife felt just as awkward.

In 1882 when they last parted, Mrs. Hart was only 35, still in the prime of her life. Now, 24 years later, she was 59, and the years had not been kind to her. Had they been living together, day in and day out as any other couple, and aged together, it would have been a natural and beautiful process. But the long years of separation had rendered them almost strangers. For two strangers to act like husband and wife called for professional acting skills. Hart was no actor but he felt obliged to try the part.

He put his wife up in another bedchamber, believing it would also have been her wish. At least all had their own private spaces. He felt that handling his relationship with his wife was not any simpler than handling diplomatic relationships.

Hart's lifestyle suddenly underwent a change. He had been used to a bachelor's life, and no longer knew how to be a husband and a father. In a way he had become quite an oddity. Yes, an oddity, an automaton, a bore. Living by himself, he needed only fifteen minutes for lunch and twenty minutes for supper. It was very simple. Eating was out of necessity rather than for enjoyment. And now, with another chance at family life, he had lost the ability to enjoy what it had to offer.

Now, a whole hour had to be devoted to lunch and one and a half hours for dinner! He used to spend an hour before supper writing letters and two hours after supper reading. Now he had to give the hours over to chatting with his family. This should have been a pleasure. How had it become a burden? Even he was frightened at the thought that he was no longer a normal human being. Of course he would not let on his true feelings to his wife and daughter. But he could sense that his wife's feelings were not much different from his, and this brought him a little comfort.

His wife and daughter also brought with them a host of other obligations. Before he had been able to turn down any number of society functions, including those held at diplomatic legations and with Chinese officials. Now he no longer had excuses to get out of them. Worse still, the lonely wives of the diplomats took Mrs. Hart's arrival as justification for throwing parties. Invitations showered on the Harts like snowflakes. Hart felt that his time was no longer his own and even his health was affected. But above all he thought, "After two dozen years of solitariness, I don't run as easily in a 'double harness' as I would have done had I been at it all the time!"[67]

Mrs. Hart also felt exhausted and overburdened. They had something in common on this point. She had come on this visit to perform her duty. Now that she had done that, she thought she had acquitted herself quite well. The plan was to stay for only a little more than one month in China so they had bought train tickets to depart on April 23. They were to go to Hankou from Beijing and then take steam passages from Hankou to San Francisco via Shanghai and Japan. They were packed and ready to go when on April 18, a major earthquake hit San Francisco. The following day, a fire broke out that almost burned down the entire city. Given this sudden natural disaster, there was nothing for it but to unpack and stay on.

Chapter Eleven

On May 9, 1906, the Chinese imperial court issued an edict that would shake Hart's world. It appointed Tieliang, Secretary of the Department of Revenue, and Tang Shaoyi, Assistant Secretary of the Board of Foreign Affairs, as Administrators-General of Tax Revenues. All employees of the Customs, Chinese and foreign, were to report to them.

Holding the scroll with the imperial edict, Hart found his hands were trembling. His mind as sharp as ever, he knew that this edict was no ordinary one. The Customs had always been under the Zongli Yamen, and Hart had a high degree of autonomy over what was virtually his independent kingdom. With the appointment of new tax administrators, Hart now had two bosses. "All employees of the Customs, Chinese and foreign, were to report to them" meant that Hart was deprived of the power to independently manage Customs business. The Chinese government had taken back power over the Customs. This was a sea change.

Hart had in fact long seen it coming. Many years earlier, he had proposed promoting some Chinese employees but the Qing government had turned down his request. However, he was clear-headed enough to see that having the Chinese managing their own Customs was something that was bound to happen. To rely on foreigners to guard their front gate was out of necessity rather than choice. He had always thought that he could wait calmly for that day to come. Now that the day was here, he found himself anything but calm.

How could this have happened? Hart had been vociferously claiming that he was getting old and it was time for him to go, but before he was even gone, his status at the Customs had been changed. He reproached himself for having brought all this about. Just think, for the last few years, he had not stopped asking for home leave. While trying to talk him into staying, the Qing government must have at the same time been considering what to do after his departure. Would another foreigner have his skills in managing relationships and in safeguarding Chinese interests? Customs services were so important to China that of course a proper plan was needed. Then he remembered what Prince Qing had asked him when the problem of succession first came up: "Why can't we look for a Chinese?"

Who was to blame?

In fact there was a larger picture involved.

The 1901 Treaty was second to none in heaping humiliation on China. The shame of ceding territory and paying indemnities fueled the patriotic passion of the Reformists and revolutionaries, leading to a national awakening. The domestic class conflicts deepened until they became irreconcilable. In order to hold on to her precarious rule, the Empress Dowager Cixi felt compelled to engage in reforms.

In the three years since she had returned to Beijing from Xi'an, she announced three new policies: 1. Advocating and encouraging private industrial enterprises; 2. Abolishing the civil service examination system, establishing schools and encouraging studies abroad; and 3. Restructuring the military and organizing a new-style army. These new policies had not yet played a role in stabilizing the political situation. But as they were implemented, Western-educated people were appointed to office and, forming a new force in the government, they set their sights on the Customs Service, which was at the peak of its power under a foreign I. G.

The year 1903 witnessed the establishment of the Board of Commerce, the first institution founded under the new policies. Soon thereafter, it began to share power with the Customs and was to take over the trademark registration right, but objections from foreign legations stopped it from taking effect.

And then there was the 1904 World Fair incident. The Chinese Customs had always been responsible for selecting items from China to showcase at World Fairs. At the 1904 World Fair in St. Louis, the Chinese pavilion was truly bizarre, showing images of sickly women with bound feet, prisoners, beggars, prostitutes and opium-smokers. The magazine *The Eastern Miscellany*, newly launched by the Shanghai Commercial Press, carried articles vehemently condemning the selections. Expatriate students and merchants abroad also wrote to the Waiwu Bu [the new Board of Foreign Affairs] to express their indignation, and proposed that selections of Chinese exhibits for the 1905 World Fair in Italy should be made by Chinese. Yang Beijun, Qing ambassador to Belgium, submitted a memorandum to the throne, saying that as exhibits selected by foreigners were often inappropriate and liable to becoming laughingstocks, the Board of Commerce should, in the future, assign the job to officials in charge of commerce, who would work in conjunction with Chinese emissaries in the countries where World Fairs were to be held. Thus, the Board of Commerce and the Board of Foreign Affairs jointly petitioned the imperial court, and with the court's approval, the Board of Commerce took over from the Customs the right to select items for future World Fairs.

These two incidents were preludes, signals of changes to come. In fact, efforts to take back the Customs' rights had been going on behind the scenes well before the issuance of the edict of May 9.

The strongest reaction to the new edict came from the British Legation. That very day, Cecil Carnegie, chargé d'affaires of the British Legation reported to the British Foreign Office about the edict, saying that everyone was shocked and worried about its possible consequences. Then he rushed over to see Hart for his take.

Hart sat quietly smoking without saying a word. He had already calmed down after the initial shock. At 71 years of age, he had enough political experience not to look agitated although the edict had everything to do with him. Serenely he told the chargé d'affaires to wait and see rather than speaking out too early.

But the pressure on him was all too evident, particularly at a moment when the air was full of rumor about his departure. Objectively speaking, this arrangement in advance of Hart's departure was not only unsurprising but actually wise. With Tieliang and Tang Shaoyi in charge of Customs affairs, the question of succession would lose its urgency. And lowering the status of his successors was a very reasonable and logical approach. He noted, "If I were to feel huffed and resign right off, there would be an amount of confusion that would work mischief immediately, but, if I take it quietly I may perhaps knead matters into proper form and condition. ... The foreign inspectorate is entering on a transformation period, with results to come that will be seriously felt as time goes on."[68]

The British Foreign Secretary Edward Grey's reply telegram to the chargé d'affaires was in the arrogant tone of a true colonialist. It instructed Carnegie to notify the Chinese government that if the edict was meant to undercut the power of the I.G., it would be a violation of the guarantees given by the Chinese government in the Loan Agreements of 1896 and 1898.

On May 19, the foreign legations in China convened a special meeting to discuss the situation resulting from the imperial edict and decided to support Britain in its protests.

It was after careful consideration that the Qing government had taken this step. However strong the reaction of the other side, the Chinese leaders remained unflustered and composed. It was not until the fourth day after the issuance of the edict that the newly appointed tax administrators Tieliang and Tang Shaoyi met Hart.

They were all politeness to him. This foreigner had worked in China for 51 years, and as head of the Customs for 45. It is rare in any country to have one official holding sway over a key government department for so long. In Hart's case, this was a demonstration of the Qing government's confidence in him. The two ministers assured him that the edict meant nothing more than that Hart must report to them in addition to reporting to the Foreign Affairs Board, and probably in some cases, report only to them. Otherwise, all would remain the same as before.

Hart summarized, "They received me nicely enough and talked nicely, but of course sceptics are in the majority and say that as soon as they are in the saddle they will ride at their pace and in their own direction, and sooner or later this will probably be the case, but I think later rather than sooner, and, for the present, we shall have peace and quiet. This is, however, the beginning of the end and some day China will take complete control and foreigners disappear from all except very subordinate posts. Meantime the Legations are much exercised—but their activity will, I fear, do more harm than good, for their views are not identical and one of them, the German, if not encouraging Chinese action, stands aloof, and this 'rift' will spoil the 'music!' Much more depends on my coolness and temper than on outside intervention. ... I had hoped for no change in my time, but Tieh said yesterday they wish to have a working control established as a going concern before I disappear and as they said, though nobody wants me to go except those who would like to fill my place, it is known I cannot hold on for ever, and the disorganization likely to follow an unprepared-for departure should be avoided."[69]

However, reason and emotion are quite different things. Hart remained restless, with little interest in doing what lay outside of his daily routine. The weather in May of that year was chillier than usual. The lovely blue-sky mornings were followed by brown, dusty, windy afternoons, and the temperature fluctuated. Maybe it was only Hart's imagination, but he felt that even the weather was out to get him.

As only to be expected, the imperial edict caused quite a stir in the Customs Service. At such an unstable moment, it was not possible for Hart to leave. But his wife had decided to leave Beijing, departing on May 28 on a route that would take her first to Hankou. Then she would probably stay for two weeks each in Japan and the United States, and return to England in August or earlier.

With regard to Carnegie's protests, Prince Qing dragged his feet and didn't send a reply until June 1, saying that the edict in no way changed the customs administration specified in the Loan Agreements. As for the American Minister's protests, Tang Shaoyi told him right out, "Since the I. G. is employed by China, the Chinese government has the right to keep his actions under its control."

This was not the end of the matter. The Qing government carried out its established policy in an orderly fashion. On July 22, Tieliang and Tang Shaoyi, in the name of "the Administrators-General of Tax Revenues, Grand Councilor, Secretary of the Board of Revenues, and Assistant Secretary of the Foreign Affairs Board," sent a letter to the Inspector General. It announced the establishment of the Tax Office and said that all future business of the Customs at the various port cities was to fall within the purview of the new Tax Office, excepting cases involving foreign affairs, which were to be referred to the Board of Foreign Affairs, and the dispensation of tax revenues, which were to be referred to the Board of Revenue. Two days later, the Board of Foreign Affairs also addressed a letter to the I. G. saying that all matters relating to taxes and reports thereon from the Customs of the various ports were to be submitted directly to the Tax Office. Soon, the Tax Office—which had more than twenty officials transferred to it from the Board of Revenue and the Board of Foreign

Affairs, as well as some high-level Chinese employees from the Customs with a wealth of experience—started its work in an orderly manner.

The setting up of a Tax Office to take over the Foreign Affairs Board's jurisdiction over the Customs was a move of far-reaching significance. On the one hand, with this government agency devoted exclusively to managing the Customs, the Customs' independence was watered down and the scope of its power was narrowed. On the other hand, and more importantly, the relationship between the I. G. and the Foreign Affairs Board was severed, to stop Hart from interfering in China's foreign affairs and to abolish the Customs' unique and privileged status.

When the edict to set up the Tax Office was issued, Hart was on vacation at Beidaihe. He had a dip in the sea every morning before nine and walked in the hills, four or five miles in the evening between six and eight o'clock, before taking his supper by the sea.

His days were leisurely enough, but his mind knew no peace. As he stood by the sea listening to the waves lapping against the shore, this elderly Irishman well-versed in Chinese culture would often be filled with grief recalling timeless lines chanted at this spot more than 1,700 years ago by the warlord and poet Cao Cao, whose work reflected on the ephemeral nature of life. Judging from his experience, Hart sensed that more changes were on the way.

He returned to Beijing in early September. On September 8, 1906, he visited the Tax Office for the first time. To his surprise, neither Tieliang nor Tang Shaoyi showed up. He was instead met by two Chinese officials transferred there from the Customs. Not long ago, they had been Hart's subordinates but had now risen to become representatives of his superiors. To have these two meet Hart was by no means a careless oversight nor was it just another case of giving someone the cold shoulder. It was a deliberate act of taunt and humiliation.

His facial muscles kept quivering. When had he, a high-level diplomatic advisor to the government and honored guest of top officials, ever been subjected to such treatment! Ever since he first met Prince Gong in 1861, he had always enjoyed special status. He had access to the Empress Dowager and could associate and chat with the highest administrative officials, enjoying a status higher than that of cabinet ministers. After 45 years of devoted service to the Qing empire, it pained his heart to be put down like this in his declining years.

After returning to his residence, he closed his door to all visitors and tried to heal his wounds with loneliness. By the time he wrote to Campbell the following evening, he had calmed down and recovered from the initial overwhelming sense of humiliation. But his pain was still palpable in the letter: "The visit helped me to realise what a change the transfer from Wai-Wu-Pu makes: the advent of the Ch'u [the Tax Office] means the exit of the I. G. A new man who has not my fifty years Yamen experiences behind him will not be specially embarrassed by the changed status the transfer will be found to have involved."[70]

During Hart's sojourn at Beidaihe, Reuters reported from Beijing about his retirement. It caused a sensation in Britain. It was said the source of the news could be traced back to a letter to a friend when Hart was in Beidaihe, saying that he needed to make arrangements for his retirement to Britain. Another possible source of the news was a deliberate hint on the part of the Chinese government. At the time, even Hart himself didn't know for sure whether the Chinese government wanted him to stay on or to volunteer resignation. When leaving Beidaihe at the end of August, he was still unable to make up his mind. But after that visit to the Tax Office, things were clearer: "It has an element of bitterness in it that would make my daily cup of duty too distasteful I fear, and so I have no intention of staying longer than Easter—but, in fact, health may force me away sooner."[71]

A week later, Tang Shaoyi saw him by way of pacifying

him. They had a heart-to-heart talk. Tang told Hart that "he could not recognise or admit any foreign right to interfere in China's domestic affairs but that, between ourselves—him and me—both Customs' men, he thought it would be well for me to issue a Circular telling the Service that I am on the same footing as before—only that the Head Office is now the Shui Wu Ch'u [Tax Office], and not the Wai-Wu-Pu—that I am to carry on as before—that the Commissioners and Post Staff are on the same footing as before in relation to the I. G.—and that they are to carry on as before. Further he asked me to tell the Staff to keep silence—not to stir up discussion and bad language by giving vent to fears and apprehensions in talk or writing, seeing that such language does more harm than good and hurts the dignity of China: that China had always treated her foreign employés well, and that, so far from changing that treatment now, the desire is to do the best work for China by keeping the foreigners as required and by treating them so well that they, contented, will work heartily and do good service for China, etc., etc., etc. I had said 'China for the Chinese' is the ideal of the day and cannot be objected to, but ought to be worked up to soberly and slowly, etc., and he said 'Yes—China for the Chinese is a thing that must be recognized, but also it must not be exaggerated.'"[72]

This conversation worked well. The Chinese government handled this momentous affair with consummate political skill. While dealing Hart a blow, it also soothed him. While declaring its stand and leaving no doubt as to the direction of future developments, it did nothing to affect the normal functioning of the Customs. Truth be told, the Chinese government was not yet ready to take over all the operations of the Customs but the timing of the edict, while Hart was still the I. G., could not have been better.

After that conversation, Hart drafted a circular and cleared it with Tieliang and Tang Shaoyi before issuing it. Being the sensible man he was, Hart was going to act wisely so as to weather the storm and wrap up his career in peace:

"An end will come some day, sooner if we or our 'friends' act foolishly, and later if we are fairly efficient in work, and act wisely."[73]

The ripples caused by the May 9 edict having subsided for the time being, an old problem again rose to the surface. It was the problem of a successor to Hart. Succession had always been a major force of rivalry in Chinese officialdom. To the credit of those fighting over the future of the important I. G. post, it did not come to blows and was civilized enough. But it was indeed a complicated case involving not only personal interests but also multiple national interests.

In the fall of 1906, Hart told the newly appointed British Minister Jordan that he planned to return to Britain in the following spring and recommended that Robert Bredon take over his job. To his inquiry about the British government's attitude, Jordan replied that as Bredon was not popular in or outside of the Customs, the British government did not think he was the right candidate. From another channel, Hart heard that the Chinese government was not satisfied with Bredon either and thought Alfred E. Hippisley the best candidate. So in January 1907, Hart felt obliged to indicate that during his vacation, he would recommend three candidates for the Chinese government to choose from.

Nevertheless he did not return to his home country in the spring of 1907 as he had indicated. He wanted to make a last effort to put the question of succession to rest. In the spring, he again announced that Robert Bredon was the best candidate in his estimation and, at the same time, he transferred Hippisley to Beijing as the Commissioner of Postal Services, hoping to achieve a balance in so doing. He himself was still being swamped by work.

His closest old friend Campbell had recently undergone surgery for intestinal obstruction, after which his health took a turn for the worse. In June the doctors informed him that there was no hope for a recovery, and he died on December 3, 1907. It was then that Hart made up his mind to leave

China. On January 27, 1908, the Emperor granted him one year of leave of absence and, in the same decree, approved his recommendation of Robert Bredon, but only as the Acting I. G.

On the day of Hart's departure from Beijing, he left a note on his desk: "Lubin Hart left at 7:00 am, April 13, 1908." He knew that he was not to return.

The Beijing Railway Station echoed with drum music. The platform was thronged with people there to see him off. The curtain fell with a festive ambience.

The Finale

When Hart returned home, to a country he had not seen in thirty years, he was greeted with honors and respect.

Oxford University offered him a doctorate in civil law, the University of Dublin an honorary LL.D., and his alma mater appointed him as Pro-Chancellor. London, Belfast and the Borough of Taunton all extended him honorary citizenship. He went to banquets, granted interviews, and found himself amid flowers and applause. But as only to be expected, the excitement was temporary. When life returned to normal, he realized that he was outside its tracks. His career was in China. China was the source of his glory and pride. Britain had nothing to do with him, other than as the place of his birth.

Less than six months after Hart's return home, the Empress Dowager Cixi and Emperor Guangxu died at almost the same time. As the dynasty for which he had done a lifetime of service tottered on its last legs, he was stricken with the grief of an official serving a nation on the verge of collapse. But he was in no position to turn the tide.

His first and foremost concern was his successor, who was to lead the Customs kingdom that he had created single-handedly. He still insisted on Robert Bredon in spite of objections from both the Chinese and British governments. In a final attempt, he sent telegrams to the Foreign Affairs Board and the Tax Office on November 22, 1909, saying he was preparing to return to China by sea to resume his office. But he fell gravely ill prior to departure. By January, he knew he had to abandon Robert Bredon. He recommended five candidates to the Chinese government, which then picked Francis Arthur Aglen, the first on his list. The Qing government did so to give him "face," because Aglen's father had been Hart's schoolmate.

On April 15, 1910, Aglen succeeded Bredon as the Acting I. G. and in June was appointed as the Executive I. G. As long as Hart was alive, the Chinese government made a point of keeping the title of I. G. solely for him.

On September 20, 1911, Hart passed away in Buckinghamshire, at age 77. On September 23, the Chinese Emperor issued a decree, posthumously promoting him to Senior Guardian of the Heir Apparent. This was the highest honor a foreigner could be granted in China.

Three weeks later, the dynasty that had granted this honor to Hart also came to an end.

Translators' Notes

1. Later known as Queen's University Belfast
2. The Priesthill Methodist Church
3. Phrases in the text that appear in italics are Robert Hart's own words, as taken from various publications and correspondence. Longer direct quotes are in quotations marks with references. The words here were quoted in *A Tale of Two Churches: Two Centuries of Methodism at Priesthill 1786 – 1996*, Chapter 8. www.lisburn.com/books/priesthill.8.html. Also see Bruner, K F, Fairbank, J K, & Smith, R J, eds., *Entering China's Service: Robert Hart's Journals, 1854 – 1863*. Council on East Asian Studies, Harvard University, 1986, p. 6.
4. *Entering China's Service*, p. 23.
5. Ibid., p. 63.
6. An establishment used by a Chinese government official or department for business and often also as a residence
7. *Entering China's Service*, p. 185.
8. Ibid.
9. Ibid., p. 186.
10. Ibid.
11. Ibid., p. 218.
12. Smith, Richard J., Fairbank, John K, Bruner, Katherine F ed., *Robert Hart and China's Early Modernization: His Journals, 1863 – 1866* Harvard University Press: Cambridge (Massachusetts) and London, 1991, p.428.
13. Fairbank, John King, Bruner, Katherine Frost, Matheson, Elizabeth M., ed., *The I. G. in Peking: Letters of Robert Hart Chinese Maritime Customs 1868 – 1907 Vol. 1*, pp. 193-4.
14. An inland tax levied upon merchandise, native and foreign.
15. Lay, Horatio Nelson "Our Interests in China." Quoted in Hsu, Immanuel. *The Rise of Modern China*. Oxford University Press: New York and Oxford, 2000. p. 277.

16. An example is Gordon's Ever-Victorious Army, which consisted of Chinese soldiers who fought for the Qing Dynasty against the rebels, but were trained and led by a European officer corps.

17. Lay, Horatio Nelson. "Our Interests in China." Quoted in *The Journal of International Relations*, Vol. 8, Clark University: Worcester MA, p. 422.

18. *The I. G. in Peking*, p. 234.

19. Tiffen, Mary. *Friends of Sir Robert Hart: Three Generations of Carrall Women in China*. Tiffania Books: East Sussex, UK. p. 92.

20. *The I. G. in Peking*. Vol. 1, p. 205.

21. Ibid., p. 300.

22. Ibid., p. 515.

23. Ibid., p. 575.

24. Ibid., p. 583.

25. Ibid., p. 590.

26. Ibid., p. 592.

27. *The I. G. in Peking*, Vol. 2, p. 869.

28. Ibid., p. 878.

29. Ibid., p. 900.

30. Ibid., p. 922.

31. An old word for "burdens"

32. *The I. G. in Peking*, p. 928.

33. Ibid., p. 929.

34. Ibid., p. 955.

35. Ibid., p. 955.

36. Ibid., p. 956.

37. Jiawu refers to the way the year 1894 is called under the traditional Chinese cyclical calendar.

38. *The I. G. in Peking*, p. 984.

39. Ibid., p. 993.

40. Ibid., p. 1021. This was Hart's assessment of his daughter-in-law in a subsequent letter to Campbell.

41. Ibid., p. 1062.

42. Ibid., p. 1073.

43. Ibid., p. 1078.

44. Ibid., p. 1092.

45. Ibid., p. 1188.

46. Ibid., p. 1198.
47. Ibid., p. 1203.
48. Ibid., p. 1218.
49. Ibid., p. 1240.
50. Robert Hart, *These from the Land of Sinim*, Chapman & Hall: London, reprinted by the University of Michigan, 2012, p. 49.
51. *These from the Land of Sinim*, pp. 49-50.
52. Ibid., p. 51.
53. Ibid., p. 59.
54. *The I. G. in Peking*, p. 1238.
55. Ibid., pp. 141-2.
56. Ibid., p. 1248.
57. Ibid., p. 1094.
58. Ibid., p. 1094.
59. Ibid., p. 1255.
60. Ibid., p. 1280.
61. Ibid., p. 1308.
62. Ibid., p. 1308.
63. Ibid., p. 1312.
64. Ibid., p. 1444.
65. Ibid., p. 1444.
66. Ibid., p. 1481.
67. Ibid., p. 1503.
68. Ibid., p. 1506.
69. Ibid., p. 1507.
70. Ibid., p. 1517.
71. Ibid., p. 1517.
72. Ibid., p. 1518.
73. Ibid., p. 1519.